PRAISE FOR STEPHEN LEATHER

'A writer at the top of his game'
Sunday Express

'A master of the thriller genre'
Irish Times

'Let Spider draw you into his
web, you won't regret it'
The Sun

'The sheer impetus of his storytell-
ing is damned hard to resist'
Daily Express

'High-adrenaline plotting'
Sunday Express

'Written with panache, and a fine ear for dia-
logue, Leather manages the collision between
the real and the occult with exceptional skill,
adding a superb time-shift twist at the end'
Daily Mail on *Nightmare*

DROP ZONE

Hot Blood
Dead Men
Live Fire
Rough Justice
Fair Game
False Friends
True Colours
White Lies
Black Ops
Dark Forces
Light Touch
Tall Order
Short Range

Spider Shepherd: SAS thrillers :
The Sandpit
Moving Targets

Jack Nightingale supernatural thrillers:
Nightfall
Midnight
Nightmare
Nightshade
Lastnight
San Francisco Night
New York Night
Tennessee Night

DROP ZONE

A SPIDER SHEPHERD: SAS NOVELLA

STEPHEN LEATHER

CHAPTER 1

Dan "Spider" Shepherd looked around with interest as his military driver headed south through the Georgia countryside. There'd been a pile-up on the freeway so they were using lesser roads, but they were still arrow straight, passing through arid grasslands and forests, between the inevitable American mix of two blocks wide but one hundred blocks long small towns, together with strip malls, gas stations, Baptist churches and roadside eateries offering local delights such as southern fried chicken and chicken and dumplings.

Shepherd had been on several training exercises and exchanges with US Special Forces at the Delta Force compound at Fort Bragg in North Carolina, but this was his first trip into the heart of "Dixie" - the Deep South. He had flown into Atlanta, Georgia, on a commercial flight and was heading still further south towards the Alabama-Georgia border and a military base and training area that was even bigger than Fort Bragg. Fort Benning military reservation covered 180,000 acres with a total military and civilian population of 120,000 people. It was also home to an airborne division of 20,000 men, along with many other units, including the US Army Armor School, The US Army Infantry School and The Western Hemisphere Institute for Security Co-operation, that used to be known as The School of the Americas. The reservation had become notorious as the place where cold-eyed army officers from Central and South American countries - Chile, Argentina, Brazil, Paraguay, Bolivia, Nicaragua, Guatemala, Panama and many more - had come to learn the techniques and make the contacts within the higher ranks of the US military that they would later need to draw on in military coups back home. It was strongly rumoured that among the many things those Central and Southern Americans learned at the School of the Americas were the techniques of "enhanced interrogation" - though neutral observers would almost certainly have described it as torture - which those same army officers would take back home with them and later make considerable use of to root out dissent and opposition to their military juntas. Try as he might, Shepherd could not think of a single Central or South American country that had not been subverted in some way, at some time, by direct or indirect US military involvement. Legitimate, elected governments were destabilised or overthrown, rebellions and insurrections were fomented, coups orchestrated, and dictators and juntas installed or preserved in power, all in the name of freedom and democracy, of course.

They turned in past the sign at the gates reading: "Welcome to Fort Benning, Home of the Infantry." Fort Benning was also the base of the US Army Jump School, which was where Shepherd was heading. It was run by the First Battalion (Airborne) of the 507th Division, and people from all branches of the US military - not just parachute troops and not just the Army either - came there for parachute training.

Shepherd was dropped off at the Jump School's compound and was greeted by an officer wearing the badges of rank of a Brigadier-General. 'Welcome aboard,' he said, in a deep south drawl. 'So this is what one of those famous SAS men we've heard so much about actually looks like?'

'Sort of,' Shepherd said, 'but the rest of them are much better looking.'

The other man slapped him on the back. 'My name's Herman, but everybody calls me Hank. You can drop your bag right here and I'll have someone take it to your quarters while I show you around.' Hank led Shepherd across the training area to the Jump School's training towers. There were three of them, all 250-feet high, though only two appeared to be in use. The trainees were being put in a harness with a parachute already deployed, before being hauled up to the top of one of the towers and then abruptly dropped again. Even for seasoned jumpers it must have been an unsettling experience and if the white faces of the novices were anything to go by, it was truly terrifying for first-timers.

Shepherd kept glancing around and noted that, unlike his escorting officer, the training staff were predominantly African-American, and all were turned out as immaculately as the British Brigade of Guards. 'Your guys are certainly sharp dressers, Hank,' he said. 'The creases in those uniforms are so sharp you could cut yourself on them.'

Hank nodded. 'It's something we pride ourselves on here. We even break starch - put on a completely fresh uniform - twice a day: in the morning and after lunch.'

As Hank led him on a tour of the rest of the Jump School's training areas, they walked past a parade ground where the trainees had been divided into squads and were being paraded by their trainers while wearing full uniform and carrying flags. Whenever they met an officer coming the other way they all had to shout in unison 'All the way, Major' or Colonel, or whatever his rank was, and the officer would then reply with 'Above the rest, men.' It was, Shepherd privately reflected, exactly the sort of bullshit that the SAS had discarded years ago, along with marching, parades and other useless pseudo-military activities.

Shepherd was already a seasoned parachute jumper; having originally come to the SAS from the Parachute Regiment, and he had done plenty more jumps since then. The techniques that British airborne forces used were similar to those of the Americans but with a couple of crucial differences. When US airborne infantry parachuted from an aircraft there was always an interval of about 100 feet between them when they hit the ground. So ten men would be spread out over 1000 feet and 100 men would be scattered over a distance of a couple of miles.

In combat, troops were most vulnerable to attack when they had just landed and were all still acting as individuals, before they had RVed with their comrades. In the RV system used by regular soldiers, individuals progressively formed into patrols, squads, sections, platoons and then companies, and they couldn't react effectively against any attack until they had RVed with each other which, given the size of the gaps between them as they hit the ground, could take some considerable time to achieve.

In British Para and SAS training, men jumped from the aircraft much closer together: three men in every 100 feet, instead of one. It was potentially more dangerous because they were more likely to have accidental collisions in mid-air or become entangled in each other's chutes, but it meant they could RV much quicker on the ground and therefore face and deal with any enemy threats that much faster.

While serving with the SAS, Shepherd had been training in and using the HALO - High Altitude Low Opening - technique under which SAS men would jump from their aircraft at high altitude - 30,000 or even 40,000 feet - and free-fall until deploying their parachutes at as low as 3,000 feet above the ground. In order to use the technique, the aircraft they were jumping from had to be de-pressurised, with the men plugging in to the oxygen bank of a Hercules or using the aircraft's own emergency oxygen system on a commercial aircraft.

In theory it allowed the Regiment to make covert insertions in to areas that would have been barred to a British military flight. An SAS patrol could board a commercial jet using a standard flight-path for a journey from, say, Heathrow to Hong Kong. The patrol could then exit the aircraft in a HALO jump over any of the intermediate countries and in theory no one would be the wiser. However, the technique had never worked satisfactorily in practice and Shepherd felt that the Regiment's continuing experiments with the technique might have blinded them to a much better alternative. Rather than using HALO, he had been wanting to test the opposite technique - Ultra Low Level (ULL) - in which the jumper would exit the aircraft just 300 feet above the ground but still deploy his parachute in time to land safely and without injury.

He was well aware that, had he proposed the idea to the RAF, the British military bureaucracy would have meant he would have been lucky to get the go-ahead within ten years, and even then the proposal would have been tinkered with and altered so much along the way that it would no longer be recognisable as what he'd applied for. However by pitching it - with the SAS's blessing - to Delta Force instead, he could get permission, and even better, get a budget and any equipment he needed, within months or even weeks. The SAS's stellar reputation among the world's military meant that Delta Force were always happy to learn from them and without hesitation they had agreed to provide training facilities, aircraft, personnel, logistical support and a budget for contingencies. Their only stipulation was that a couple of Delta Force guys had to be part of the project, acting as observers.

When he arrived at Fort Benning's Jump School to begin testing the technique, Shepherd was immediately given the honorary rank of Warrant Officer Class 1. The peculiarities of the American rank system meant that Warrant Officers were more esteemed than most commissioned officers, even Colonels, so though he was reporting to Hank, who was a Brigadier General, he treated him pretty much as an equal and Shepherd at once became one of the most respected individuals on the base. Shepherd used the same facilities as the officers, eating in the Commissary attached to the PX, which was like a very large and extremely well-stocked supermarket. The only slight drawback was that his accommodation was in the BOQ - the Bachelor Officer Quarters - which were pretty basic compared with the normal quarters, but since Shepherd was there to work and didn't plan to be at Fort Benning for more than a couple of weeks, it suited him well enough.

After finally managing to shake off Hank, who had seemed intent on walking him around the entire 180,000 acres of the base in person, Shepherd used the rest of his first day to wander around, getting his bearings and becoming familiar with the Jump School, its facilities and its personnel. He spent a couple of hours watching the trainees going through the basic training course but then moved on to the Experienced Wing where they were training in and practising more advanced jumping procedures, though not the Ultra Low Level technique that Shepherd was pioneering. ULL jumping had actually started way back in the 1930s, when it was first developed by the Russians. They practised exiting from aircraft flying at very low level and jumped without any parachutes at all, hoping that a soft landing in deep snow would prevent too many injuries. That hope was not fulfilled; casualty levels were horrific, and after that, there was understandably no rush from other nations to adopt or develop the technique. Shepherd's technique was considerably safer than that of the Russians, but he had yet to prove it.

CHAPTER 2

Aconvoy of cars was lined up on the tarmac as the US Congressman came down the steps of the Gulfstream jet, one of the fleet of private jets the US government kept to fly its politicians and officials around the world. As soon as Congressman Thabo Keita had seated himself in his limousine, it swept through the airport security gates and drove south along Steve Biko Road towards the city. He was handsome with coffee coloured skin - his mother was mixed race, or Cape Coloured in the classification of the apartheid era. His father was Nigerian and they had emigrated to the US before their son was born.

South African government security men in Mercedes G-Wagon 4x4s were at the head and tail of the convoy, but American personal protection officers were also travelling in another G-Wagon just behind the black limousine - a Mercedes 500 with smoked windows - that carried the VIP passenger. If Keita had been a representative of any other nation than the United States, his own bodyguards would have been unarmed, relying on the host country's own armed security men, but in this, as in so many other things, the US chose to ignore the standard international protocols and procedures and instead wrote its own rules. So here, as in every other country in the world, the American bodyguards were armed.

Close to the city centre, the convoy turned on to Government Avenue, making for the Bryntirion Estate, the most exclusive and expensive estate in South Africa. It was still home to many of Pretoria's richest white citizens, but the nation's new black rulers now occupied the vast complex of government buildings and residences at its heart. It was surrounded by a low wire fence, capped with a coil of razor wire, and a few metres beyond it was a second, much higher fence of steel mesh on a black steel framework. Armed soldiers patrolled the perimeter and though there were several access roads, each was blocked by a steel gate, watched over by a guardpost.

A Harvard graduate, Keita had worked as a civil rights lawyer and now, still young and very ambitious, he was a US Congressman for one of the rust-belt northern states. He watched as the guard on the gate checked the credentials the driver handed to him and then spoke into his lapel mic before raising the barrier and waving the car through. They drove on, past a series of whitewashed, red-roofed villas that were home to cabinet ministers and high officials. Higher still on the hillside was the Vice-President's residence named after Oliver Tambo. Nelson Mandela's friend and contemporary, Tambo had led the ANC in exile throughout the long years of struggle with the apartheid regime and lived long enough to see its collapse before his death.

After passing a helipad, several tennis courts, a nine-hole golf course and another villa used as the Presidential guest house, they reached the government mansion, surrounded by beautiful gardens, right at the summit of the estate. Known as "Libertas" under the apartheid regime, the mansion had now been renamed *Mahlamba Ndlopfu* – The New Dawn. Its immaculate, white-painted walls and the doric columns flanking the entrance shone blindingly white in the South African sun.

As the limousine drew to a halt, Keita's American bodyguards - four near-identical figures with crew cuts, dark suits, ear pieces and permanent scowls on their features - surrounded his limousine, facing out. They checked out all possible threats before allowing him to get out, then formed a phalanx around him, elbowing the South African security men aside as they mounted the steps. The President was waiting patiently to greet him in person. He was instantly recognisable with his grizzled grey hair and vibrantly coloured "*Madiba*" shirt – Mandela's traditional clan name – one of the batik-dyed tee-shirts that he almost always wore, even to formal state occasions.

Keita and Mandela paused for the traditional handshake for the official photographer, and then Mandela led him inside. 'Quite a view,' said Keita as they settled themselves in chairs by the picture window framing the towering crags and deep ravines of the Magaliesberg mountains.

'Better than Robben Island, certainly,' Mandela said with another smile. 'So, we're your last call on a whistle-stop tour of the new African states?'

Keita nodded. 'Just aiming to build a few bridges and strengthen our ties here.'

'And keep the Chinese and Russians at bay too?'

Keita inclined his head. 'Some American aims don't change whichever party is in power.'

'So what about your own aims, Congressman? My aides tell me that you're very much a coming man among the Democrats. Might you even be living in a White House of your own one of these days?'

He held up his hand and gave a self-deprecating smile. 'With respect, I don't think the US is quite ready for a black president yet. Maybe it never will be.'

Mandela laughed. 'Come on, Congressman. If there can be a black president of South Africa, the most segregated and racist society in the world until a very few years ago, then surely there can be a black president of the United States?' He paused. 'Anyway, we'll come back to that but now, tell me about yourself and your family.'

'Well, I've a wife who's a lot cleverer than me and two daughters, who take after their mother. Matter of fact, one's here in Africa with me. She's on a safari in Zimbabwe at the moment and when I've finished my official meetings, I'm joining her for a trip to the Victoria Falls.'

'Like a lot of other things in Africa,' Mandela said, 'that name is a relic left over from colonial times that we need to reclaim for ourselves. Its African name is much more evocative: *Mosi-oa-Tunya*: "The smoke that thunders". A lot of the waters of the Zambezi are diverted for irrigation these days but the falls are still an awe-inspiring sight, especially in the wet season. They say that when conditions are right, you can see the mist and spray from fifty kilometres away.'

'Well, I'm hoping to get a bit closer than that,' said Keita.

'Then let's get down to business straight away,' Mandela said, 'and then you'll be free to go and do so.' They settled down to an in-depth discussion while the security men continued to prowl the terrace outside.

Chapter 3

When Shepherd was ready to begin trialling Ultra Low Level jumps, he was allocated his own choice of aircraft from Fort Benning's fleet and he selected a Starlifter C141. A four-engine jet with a very high tailplane, its civilian use was mainly as a commuter aircraft, but Shepherd chose it mainly because, with in-flight refuelling, it could practically fly for ever. He sited cameras on the ground and inside the aircraft to record each jump from all angles. The only other modification was to coat the fuselage behind the exit doors with coloured grease. If his chute deployed too close to the fuselage as he exited the aircraft, even if he heard or felt nothing himself - and that was unlikely given the noise and buffeting of the slipstream as he hit it - the grease marks on the chute would show up when he examined it after the jump. The two Delta Force guys had arrived but were purely observers, watching and making notes as Shepherd did the hard yards himself.

He started with a basic military issue parachute and after each jump he checked the chute carefully, not only for signs of grease on it, but for any weakness or damage. He examined the camera footage too, assessing his technique and any areas where he could improve and then began the slow, painstaking process of adapting the chute. The aim was to take out as much material as possible while still retaining sufficient lift to slow his descent. The more he took out of it, the more stable it would be, but he was working with very fine margins. If he took too much out, he would be dead or crippled, and there was no scientific method or theory he could rely on - it was simply a matter of guesswork and trial and error.

In this he was helped by one of Fort Benning's parachute riggers. It was a specialist grade within the US Army and those who worked as riggers did nothing but adjust, alter, repair and pack parachutes. The riggers fitted nylon ties of different breaking strengths on the different parts of a parachute, thus ensuring that it deployed in the correct sequence. As the jumper exited the aircraft and the strain came on to the chute, the weakest links would break first, followed by the others in sequence, ensuring that the chute deployed exactly the way it was supposed to do. By varying the strength of the ties, the riggers could also speed up or slow down the rate at which the chute deployed.

Shepherd's rigger at Fort Benning was Lula, an African-American originally from Macon, Georgia, but now living in Columbus. Shepherd soon realised that Lula knew everything there was to know about the technicalities of parachutes, so each time he came back after a jump, he just said 'Right, this is what I need now', and Lula went ahead and did it. It wasn't unusual to have a female parachute rigger. In fact both in the US and the UK there were more female riggers than men - Shepherd truly believed that they were better at the job.

'Shoot, Spider,' she said, as he reappeared after his fifth jump that day with a fresh series of requests. 'You're going to wear these damn chutes out at this rate.'

He grinned. 'Just following the Regimental motto, what we call "The Five Ps", although it's actually six if you include the swear word: "Perfect Practice Prevents Piss Poor Performance".'

He had begun by jumping from the normal height of 800 feet but his aim was always to have his chute fully deployed, having slowed him down to a safe landing speed, before the altimeter he carried showed 500 feet. He then just hung there as the chute completed the slow descent to the ground. Once he and Lula had carried out the necessary refinements to his chute, he began steadily lowering the altitude at which he was exiting the aircraft. Under a normal parachute, from a height of 800 feet or more, a jumper would hit the ground at about seventeen feet per second. On an Ultra Low Level jump, he would be hitting the ground twice as fast, but with the right technique, though it might make his teeth rattle a little, it would still be slow enough for him to avoid the risk of injury.

The only problem he had found was with the head protection he wore, which was essential on ULL jumps. He had tried the standard issue US Army kevlar helmet, but it was so heavy and bulky that it dragged his head around in the slipstream, so he was keeping an eye out for a lighter and more aerody-namic alternative.

CHAPTER 4

Kesia Keita had spent the day in company with three other tourists and her two bodyguards, on a safari through the bushland of Zimbabwe's Hwange National Park. She'd taken endless photographs of four of the "Big Five" - lions, leopards, elephants and Cape buffalo - with only the last of the five, rhinos, proving too elusive for their guide. Originally christened the Big Five by big game hunters because they were the most difficult African animals to hunt on foot, the name had now been taken up by all the safari tour operators as well, who used it to boost their list of attractions to tourists who would rather have been shot themselves than kill one of those magnificent wild creatures.

In the late afternoon they returned to the luxurious lodge at Victoria Falls where they were staying. There was a grandiose water feature in the entrance to the lodge, a curious choice of decor when one of the most beautiful natural water features in the world was only four hundred yards away. The lodge itself was a curious mix of hotel styles: part colonial villa, part African bush retreat, part anodyne international hotel and part kitsch Las Vegas casino, complete with a gaming area full of banks of whirring, clattering slot machines. Flanked by her bodyguards, she walked through the lobby and the lounge area. Both were crowded with American and North European tourists - British, Dutch, German and Swedes.

Kesia had promised her father that she would wait for his arrival the following day so that they could go and get their first sight of the Victoria Falls together, but the lodge was within earshot of them and close enough that she could see the perpetual spray from the falls rising above the trees. Both her bodyguards - a woman US Secret Service agent and her South African equivalent, who had the rooms on either side of hers - had told her not to leave the grounds of the Lodge under any circumstances and not even to leave her room without telling them. However, as her parents had already long since discovered, Kesia was a teenager who did not like being told what to do by anyone, least of all the hired help, so she quietly eased open the French windows of her room, slipped out onto the terrace and then hurried away through the grounds. One of the Lodge's security men was standing by the pedestrian gate on the river side of the property and she asked him which way to go to the world famous falls.

'Just follow the path outside the gate, Miss, it's only a few hundred yards. Be careful to stay on the path and just use the look-out points to see the falls

though, because the spray makes the rocks very slip-
pery. Oh and Miss? It'll be sunset in an hour and
there are no lights along the path, so don't stay there
too long.'

Kesia gave the bored reply beloved by teenagers
the world over: 'Whatever.' The guard let her out of
the gate and she ran off along the path, passing a
group of Japanese tourists coming the other way. She
got her first sight of the falls as she rounded a bend in
the path and came to a look-out point. A tour guide
was there with a small group of tourists, pointing
down towards the dense rainforest flanking the river
where it emerged from the foot of the falls. 'That
jungle down there is one of the only places in the
world where it rains every single day,' she heard the
guide say before he led his party away up the path.

Kesia had the falls to herself and the sight of them
took her breath away: a massive curtain of tumbling
white water that seemed to extend all the way to the
horizon. It was only just past the end of the rainy season and the river was still in spate, so millions of tons
of water were plummeting into the narrow chasm no
more than eighty yards wide, between the falls and
the sheer rock wall facing them. As she stared at the
falling water, she had the dizzying sensation that it
could almost drag her down with it. She could not
only hear the thunder of the falls, she could feel it
vibrating in the pit of her stomach. The only outlet
for the foaming waters at the foot of the falls was
through a gorge that was little wider than the chasm

that fed it. At the far end was a deep, turbulent pool, known as the Boiling Pot. Above it she could see the Victoria Falls Bridge, where a train had paused in the middle of the centre span while its tourist passengers took a battery of photographs.

At the mid-point of the walkway alongside the railway track a couple of backpackers were waiting in the shade of a stand with a corrugated iron roof while their mates queued to do a bungee jump off the bridge. For a moment Kesia was tempted to join the queue, but she knew that if her father ever got wind of it, that was one situation she was not going to be able to talk her way out of, so she shifted her gaze away from that, back towards the falls themselves. She stood there for quite some time, still awe-struck at the sight, while the sun continued to sink slowly towards the horizon. She remained there until the spray drifting around her in the cooling air began to make her shiver and then she headed back to the Lodge.

Dusk was approaching fast and it was almost dark by the time Kesia reached the gate. There was no sign of the guard but the gate was open, so she slipped through it and was making her way back towards her room when she saw her female Secret Service bodyguard pacing the terrace. She tried to duck back behind a bush, but heard her shout. 'I see you out there in the shrubbery, Kesia. You get your ass back here now!'

She sulkily made her way back to the terrace. 'You can't talk to me like that. I'm not your daughter.'

'No, you're the daughter of a US Congressman who's tasked us with the job of keeping you safe. But the person we're supposed to be protecting - you - always thinks she knows better than we do and keeps ignoring what we tell her and putting herself in danger as a result.'

'I was perfectly safe.'

'Were you? On your own, in a strange and pretty dangerous country, standing on the edge of one of the highest waterfalls in the world. If you were perfectly safe, it was more by good luck than anything else.'

Kesia shrugged. 'There was a path and the viewpoints were fenced, so I wasn't ever going to fall in.'

'You think that's the only danger? This isn't Acron, Ohio, kiddo. This is Africa. There are wild animals here and there are gangs of robbers, poachers and kidnappers, and if they came across a young unprotected American girl, well...' She paused, struggling for the words. 'Let's just say that a lot of things could happen to you and none of them would be pleasant. Now your father gets here tomorrow with his own security team, and with luck he'll keep you occupied and out of mischief from then on in, but until then-'

'You won't tell him, will you?' Kesia said. 'About this, I mean.'

'Providing you keep to the rules from now on, stay inside the lodge and promise to let me know if you leave your room for any reason, even if it's just to go to the coffee shop or the swimming pool, then no, I guess he doesn't need to be told, mainly because if I did tell him, it wouldn't just be you who would be in serious trouble. So ... deal?'

She gave a sulky nod. 'Deal.'

Kesia had dinner with her bodyguards in the restaurant that evening and then they went back to their rooms, and she spent the evening alone in hers. There was no service on her mobile phone, and when she turned on the TV, the picture was fogged with static.

CHAPTER 5

At the start of Shepherd's second week at the Jump School, he resumed his routine of jumps, evaluation, adjustment and more jumps, and he kept steadily lowering the altitude at which he was exiting the aircraft until eventually he was jumping at 300 feet with no margin for error whatsoever if anything went wrong. He got Lula to make some final small adjustments and then made several further jumps at the minimum height before he was completely satisfied.

Now that he was happy with the technicalities of the ULL jumps, he began thinking about his operational tactics. On normal jumps the jumper had his main parachute on his back and a reserve parachute strapped to his chest, but on ULL jumps there was no point in having a reserve chute because if the main one didn't deploy, you would be dead before you had time to deploy the reserve chute anyway, so Shepherd planned to jump with only the main chute. Where the reserve one would normally have been, he opted to carry the weapon he had chosen: an MP5K, fitted with a "combat string" that held it tight against his chest. The MP5 was also carried under the parachute harness, to stop it swinging up in the slipstream into the jumper's face, and as it therefore couldn't be accessed during the descent, he had also decided to carry a 9mm semi-automatic pistol holstered on his right leg, to be used for protection if he ever came under fire while descending. Since the pistol and the MP5K were the same 9mm calibre, it had the added benefit of ensuring that the ammunition was interchangeable. On his other leg he had a sheath with an ultra sharp rescue knife. It was standard issue for aircrew and had a keen enough blade to cut through anything, including the tough strands of a parachute harness if necessary.

He also had to work out the Patrol Commander's best position for ULL jumps, whether he should be first, last or in the middle of the string. He decided that when they were flying in and hit their despatch point, the aircraft's loadmaster would first kick out the patrol's four Bergens. There would not be anything fragile inside them, so they could be dropped without any chute at all, but rather than a free drop, he decided it would be better to drop the kit using a ten-foot drogue chute. That would not only reduce the impact speed with the ground slightly but it would stabilise the kit as it descended, making its landing point more predictable and therefore easier to find. As was routine, the drogue chutes would be attached to a different cable within the aircraft than the patrol's own chutes, because the tensile strength needed to support an individual jumper was easier to calculate than for a cable holding kit that might weigh anything from as little as fifty pounds to a four or five hundredweight load so it was attached to a different strong point on the aircraft's fuselage from the one securing the jumpers' cable.

Immediately the Bergens were out, the patrol would follow, with the point man going first, the signaller and the medic second and third in the string, and Shepherd last. After their rapid-fire exit from the aircraft, the patrol would probably be separated from each other by little more than fifty feet and Shepherd could RV with them simply by walking on a reciprocal heading to the aircraft. So if it had been flying due east, he would walk due west, picking up each of the patrol members in turn. They would then carry on along the same heading until they located their Bergens, and they would then be ready to begin the op.

As he gathered up his chute after his final practice jump, Shepherd nodded to himself. Unlike HALO jumping, the ULL technique actually achieved something useful. It could put a four-man patrol on the ground within fifteen seconds of exiting the aircraft and they could RV with each other and be combat ready within a couple minutes of that. No other jumping technique could get anywhere near that level of speed and efficiency, so if Shepherd had anything to do with it, ULL would become the default for all SAS ops involving insertion by parachute.

CHAPTER 6

Just before midnight that evening, a Toyota Land Cruiser pulled up alongside two African youths, who were walking aimlessly along a street on the edge of the small Zimbabwean township. It was home to the local people who earned a precarious living cooking and cleaning for the white tourists visiting Victoria Falls but it was also home to those who, like the two youths, had no jobs at all and no reason to be in bed early. 'Hey boys,' the white driver said, in a thick Afrikaner accent. He was in his mid-forties, grey-haired and grizzled. His skin was burned and wrinkled by decades of exposure to the fierce African sun, and his expression was cast in a permanent scowl.

His name was Johannes du Prez and he was a descendant of the *Voortrekkers*, the Boer pioneers who had fled British rule in the Cape Colony in the mid-nineteenth century and made "The Great Trek" to set up their own Boer states in the Transvaal, Orange Free State and Natal, driving out or subjugating the native populations in the process. Du Prez was also a ten year veteran of the *Koevoet* - the paramilitary counter-insurgency force formed by the South West Africa Police but which also included South Africans. It fought the brutal "Bush War" against the ANC's armed wing, *uMkhonto we Sizwe* - "Spear of the Nation" - that had been co-founded by Nelson Mandela in the wake of the Sharpeville Massacre: the slaughter of unarmed Africans by white policemen that finally woke the world to the evils of the apartheid system.

The name *Koevoet* - Crowbar - was a fair reflection of the tactics adopted by a force that operated unhindered by any of the usual rules of warfare and was notorious for the atrocities it perpetrated against civilians. No one had greater notoriety than Johannes du Prez, who became known as "The Beast of the Bush" in tribute to the massacres and atrocities he had committed.

The *Koevoet* had been disbanded in 1989, as required by the UN Security Council Resolution that had at last brought the fighting to an end. The war was now long over for most black and white South Africans who, whatever their initial reluctance, had come together in the Truth and Reconciliation process. But the war was not over for du Prez and his ragtag army of rebel white soldiers. They had simply ignored the ceasefire and continued to wage war on their perceived enemies, while also terrorising the civilian populations of the areas where they operated. Most of his men were veterans of the South African or South West African forces, but there were also ex-Rhodesian SAS men, former soldiers of the Portuguese colonial regimes in Angola and Mozambique, and even a couple of ageing Americans who had developed a taste for killing, rape and murder in South-East Asia, and become soldiers of fortune in Africa rather than return to their homeland at the end of the Vietnam War.

Du Prez waved a twenty dollar bill out of the open window of the Land Cruiser. 'You boys want to earn twenty dollars?'

'Each?' one of the boys said.

'You're joking aren't you? It's already more than you'd earn in a month.'

The boys eyed him warily. There were four other white men in the vehicle, one in the passenger seat and three sitting in the back, all staring silently back at them. 'What do we have to do for it?' one of the boys said.

Du Prez smiled, though his eyes remained cold and calculating. 'Nothing like the things you're probably worrying about that white men sometimes do to young black boys. It'll be the easiest twenty you'll ever earn.' He tossed them a couple of spray cans of black paint. 'Take these, go up to the Victoria Falls Lodge and spray the CCTV cameras with them. There are three, one at the entrance gates, one over the car park and one by the main door.'

'What about the guards?'

'There are only two and they're both fat, lazy and half-asleep. If they're in the way, one of you can distract them while the other one sprays the cameras.'

'How do we distract them?'

'Throw stones at them or something, whatever it takes. Jesus, do you want the money or not?'

'Yes.' The older boy held out his hand for it.

The Afrikaner shook his head. 'Oh no, you've got to do the job first. I'll be waiting here. You'll get the money when you've done it.'

The boys looked at each other and then loped off up the road towards the lodge. They were back twenty minutes later, out of breath but giggling to each other.

'Job done?' the driver said, while the rest of the men in the vehicle remained silent.

'Yes, we did it mister. One of the guards tried to chase us but like you said, he was old and fat, so he gave up after a few yards.'

'You did all the cameras?'

'Yes, all of them. Can we have our money now?'

'Sure.' The Afrikaner beckoned them towards him and put his hand down the side of the seat but when he brought it up again, it held not the twenty dollar bill, but a silenced pistol. He fired twice, the noise of each shot no louder than a closing car-door, and both boys sprawled in the dirt, blood spurting from the holes punched in their chests. The Afrikaner in the passenger seat and one of the men in the rear got out of the Land Cruiser and dragged the bodies into the ditch alongside the road. They would be found at first light but they would be long gone by then. They got back into the

Land Cruiser and headed up the hill towards the lodge.

As they reached the lodge, the three men in the back reached down and picked up the AK47s that had been hidden by their feet. Another Land Cruiser had been waiting in a side-road, and that now swung out and followed them. It also contained five white ex-soldiers, all rangy, grizzled looking men, and all similarly armed.

The guard at the front of the lodge had barely finished grumbling to the night manager and re-taken his seat just outside the entrance door, when the Land Cruisers pulled into the car park. 'Now what the he-?' the guard said beginning to prise himself out of his chair. There was a Phttt! Phttt! sound and he pitched forward into the dirt, while a pool of dark blood began to form around his head. Two of the Afrikaners ran around the side of the building and a moment later the muffled sound of another double report from a silenced weapon showed that the other guard, stationed at the back of the lodge, had also been taken care of.

Two raiders remained outside, first severing the telephone cables and then keeping watch while the rest moved swiftly and silently through the entrance. The night manager looked up from the reception desk, blanched and reached for the alarm button, but he was shot before he could touch it, the first round smacking into his chest. His right eye then rolled up into his head as a second shot drilled through his left one and spread his brains all over the rear wall. Two of the men then ran through to the bar and disposed of the night chef and the room service waiter who had been playing cards at one of the tables.

Meanwhile one of the other gunmen had vaulted over the desk. He scanned down the entries in the hotel register until he found the one he wanted. 'Seventeen,' he said. 'So the bodyguards will be in sixteen and eighteen.'

He lifted three duplicate keys from the rack behind the reception desk. Key cards had not yet replaced the old-fashioned lock and key system here, though it would have made little difference anyway; a locked door would not have been allowed to stand between these men and their target.

While two raiders waited, weapons poised, another one slid the key silently into the lock of room eighteen and turned it. The door opened and the two raiders stepped quietly into the room. The South African security guard never even woke up as one of them drilled a hole through her forehead at point-blank range.

The other raiders were trying the same manoeuvre on room sixteen but this time the security chain was on the inside and the noise of it rattling woke the US Secret Service agent. She jumped out of bed, scrabbling for the weapon on her bedside table and calling out 'Stop or I'll shoot!'

Two silenced rounds punched through the bedroom door and then one of the raiders gave the door a savage boot, tearing the feeble security chain free. The Secret Service agent got off one shot, hitting the first raider in the gut as he launched himself through the door, but the second one fired a burst from his AK47 that ripped her body apart.

Kesia had woken at the sound of her bodyguard's door being splintered and heard the burst of gunfire, but she was still sitting up in bed, the covers pulled up to her chin as if trying to shield herself, when her door swung open and two raiders burst into the room. Her scream was cut off as one slapped her viciously across the face. Rough hands seized her wrists and ankles and cable-tied them, a piece of tape was stuck over her mouth and a hood dropped over her head. She felt herself being picked up bodily and carried out of the room.

The noise had now roused the other guests but most stayed locked in their rooms, quaking with fright, and those brave or foolhardy enough to put their noses outside their doors were greeted with a stun grenade and a burst of firing that killed two more people and sent the others diving for cover.

Carrying their hostage and their wounded comrade, the raiders ran back through the lodge, the last one pausing to send two tear gas canisters rolling down the corridor to keep the guests occupied a little longer. They piled into the Land Cruisers and drove off. From the moment they drove into the car park until the time they left again had taken no more than four minutes.

There were border posts at either end of the Victoria Falls bridge, but the one at the Zimbabwe end was closed and unmanned. The Zambian post at the other end was manned and an armed border guard stood up as he heard the sound of approaching vehicles, but his rifle was still lowered with the safety catch on as they reached him. He was cut apart by a burst of gunfire from the back of the first Land Cruiser and was dead before the sound of the Toyota had faded into the darkness as they sped away.

CHAPTER 7

At the end of his Fort Benning training, Shepherd flew to the Delta Force compound inside Fort Bragg in North Carolina. They had sponsored his training and one of the conditions was that, in company with the two Delta Force operatives who had been acting as observers, he had to report back to them at the end of his experiments with ULL jumps. While he was there, the compound went into lockdown. It was a routine procedure but a sign that something was brewing, somewhere in the world, that might require a Delta Force intervention. From the terse snatches of conversation between his Delta comrades that he overheard, Shepherd picked up that it was a hostage situation with a VIP kidnapped somewhere in Africa, but, just like the SAS, Intel in Delta Force was shared on a need to know basis, and since Shepherd didn't, he wasn't told anything else.

After finishing his debrief, he was helicoptered to Washington and then caught the regular RAF diplomatic flight from there to Brize Norton in Oxfordshire. There he was picked up by Taffy, an ex-military guy whose job as a civilian driver ferrying SAS men and senior officers around meant that he knew all the gossip.

'All right Spider?' he said as Shepherd got into the car. 'Something must be brewing because I've been told to take you straight to the PATA.'

The PATA - the Pontrilas Army Training Area - had once been a secure storage facility for high explosive munitions produced at the Rotherwas armaments factory just outside Hereford. It had been used during both world wars but by the 1960s it was surplus to requirements and was offered to the SAS. Their cramped Hereford base at Stirling Lines had no room for outdoor training and in any case, the associated gunfire and explosions would have caused considerable friction with their civilian neighbours just beyond the perimeter fence, so the Regiment jumped at the chance to acquire the PATA. It was only a dozen miles from Hereford, just outside the village of Ewyas Harold.

The job of converting it from storing high explosive munitions to an SAS base was a huge one. The storage bunkers were vast structures with thick concrete walls and massive steel doors and the cost of adapting them and building the necessary barracks and other buildings was so huge that, to justify the expense, it was designated as an Army Training Area and included in the MoD booklet circulated to all units of the British armed forces that gave details of all training areas and their facilities. In theory any other unit in the British Army could make a booking for the PATA but in practice, if anyone other than the SAS tried to do so, the training area was never available. The whole site was guarded by armed MoD police and a resident flock of geese and the standard joke among SAS men was that the geese were a lot more alert and reliable than the cops..

The buildings on the site were surrounded by a mixture of woodland and pasture covering an irregular-shaped area of about six square kilometres, but it was not ideal as a training area because of one glaring issue: a public road, Elm Tree Road, that ran straight through the site, separating one third of it from the other two thirds. The Regiment had made constant attempts to have the road closed but each time the local farmers and residents complained vociferously that closing it would force them into a twelve mile detour and cause serious problems when the river flooded, so it still remained open to anyone. There was also an old railway track that had once connected the facility to the Rotherwas armaments factory but, though the track bed still remained visible, the railway had long since been closed and the rails lifted.

The SAS had resolved the problem of the public road as best they could by using two of the three bunkers in the smaller area on the south-east side as the base for the BG - bodyguard - training cell, and the Comms - communications - team, their base being surrounded by a formidable array of aerials and satellite dishes. The other bunker had originally been used as the site for Resistance to Interrogation training, but there were strong rumours that it was now the place where captured terrorists were taken for actual interrogation, that might or might not have included techniques that Amnesty International and the Council for Civil Liberties would definitely not have approved of.

On the other side of the road, the remaining two thirds of the site contained the main SAS facilities, including an airstrip, the indoor and outdoor firing ranges, the bunker housing the Regiment's armoury and its ammunition reserves that were kept on site so there was never a risk of delay in obtaining supplies from anywhere else. There were also a couple of full-size civilian aircraft that were no longer flightworthy but were used in training for the CT - Counter-Terrorist - team. The last and by no means the least of the significant facilities at the PATA was the War Bunker where the CO of the SAS or another senior officer and his team were based during any active service op.

The whole Pontrilas Army Training Area was used 24/7 by the CT team and at any hour of the day or night, there could be explosions, bursts of firing, the clatter of helicopter rotors and the drone of Hercs or C141s flying in and out. Even though all the training activities were carried on out of direct sight of the public road, passage along it could still be an anxious business for civilians of a nervous disposition, because of the constant sounds of nearby explosions and gunfire.

The War Bunker was the place from where, if he wished to be involved, the CO could micro-manage SAS ops which, as Shepherd cynically remarked to his mates, was always the case if the CO thought there might be another medal in it for him at the end of the op. In the army tradition, medals were awarded to senior men on behalf of the others serving under them, so no matter who carried out an op, the officer was always going to get the gong. The CO, or in his absence, the ranking officer, always had a small team around him, an Ops Officer, another very senior Major, an Intelligence Officer and a driver/gofer - a man of military retirement age but who preferred to remain involved with the Regiment in some capacity. There was also one of the Army's cypher clerks - geniuses who could deal with any problems with cyphers and code. They were very necessary because if there was a problem with any tiny part of a code, the whole message would be corrupted and unreadable, so the cypher clerk's job was mainly to sort out any incomprehensible incoming or outgoing messages.

The Ops Officer and the senior Major also had their own small teams, and as well as the operational facilities, the War Bunker contained everything that was needed to remain there as long as an op lasted, including bedrooms, showers and a kitchen. Despite its importance, the War Bunker did not have any additional guards beyond those around the perimeter of the whole site, but it was clearly understood by everyone using the PATA that if you went near the War Bunker for any reason other than an invitation from the CO, your military career would be finished.

Taffy stopped at the gates while the MoD guards checked his and Shepherd's ID and then he drove him straight to the War Bunker. Shepherd walked in through the steel blast doors and went down the ramp to the War Bunker, deep below ground. The CO - a twenty-year veteran of the SAS with steel grey hair and pale blue eyes - gave him a brief nod and got straight to the point. 'We'll debrief your ULL experiment when things quieten down again, Spider, but something more urgent has cropped up. Delta Force have requested a joint op with us to free a civilian, a teenage American girl who's been abducted in Southern Africa.'

'Yeah, I heard a few whispers about that at Fort Bragg,' Shepherd said.

'Well, first of all, though it probably doesn't need saying, we're not even going to consider doing a joint-op with them. We may do similar training, et cetera, but the complexities of joint ops - political, cultural and every other damn way - are just not something I want to be having to deal with, at least in the short term and with luck, maybe never.'

'Fair enough,' Shepherd said. 'So instead you've proposed that we do the op, but with their support?'

'No,' the CO said. 'I haven't, not yet anyway, because to be honest, I don't want the bloody job. With the exception of the Counter-Terrorist Team who, as you know, have to be on permanent stand-by here in case of a terrorist incident, the other Sabre Squadrons are already abroad on ops. So the only way to do this would be to bring some of them back from overseas and, given the importance of the ops they're on, that's something I'm very reluctant to do. Which is making things a little awkward because the SIS are pushing very hard for us to accommodate the US request.'

Shepherd nodded. The SIS, also known as MI6, were always trying to use the Regiment in further-ance of the government's political aims, strength-ening alliances, creating debts and obligations, or intervening to weaken or destabilise hostile govern-ments, and even facilitate coups. It had happened enough times in the past - more than one Middle Eastern ruler owed his throne to the SAS - and no doubt would continue to do so in the future.

'And speaking of which,' the CO went on, press-ing a button on his intercom and speaking into it. 'Would you ask Mr Parker to join us now, please?'

Shepherd stifled a groan. He had met Jonathan Parker on several previous occasions. His professed occupation was as a commodities trader in the Third World, 'a little import-export, old boy,' as he liked to say, playing up the clichéd image of the English gentleman abroad - but although there was a genuine company with published accounts that would survive any audit or forensic accountant's scrutiny, it was merely a cover for Parker's work as an MI6 operative. Shepherd had formed an instant dislike for him at their first meeting in Sierra Leone when his patrol had been tasked with retrieving a botched operation that Parker had been supervising. There had been no love lost between them then and nothing he had seen of Parker since then had done anything to change his mind.

A few moments later, the man himself strolled in, nodding to Shepherd as he took a seat. He was tall and had a languid, slightly distracted air, but his keen gaze missed nothing going on around him, and he had the effortless self-confidence that an expensive public school education always seemed to instil in its pupils, whatever their talents - or lack of them. Their previous meetings had been in the Tropics, where Parker was always to be found wearing a Panama hat and an immaculate cream linen suit and white shirt, often set off with his "eggs and bacon" MCC tie, but now back in Britain, he had changed that for a traditional pin-striped business suit. Both his suit and shirt were hand-tailored, and Shepherd was amused to note that the carefully folded, lemon-coloured handkerchief in his top pocket formed a matching set with his tie and socks.

Parker nodded at Shepherd. 'Nice to see you again, I've been hearing good things about you,' he said. 'Anyway, we've no time for small talk so I'll get straight down to it. The job is to conduct a below the radar mission to find and free a hostage being held by kidnappers in Southern Africa. As you know, as a result of HM government having backed the wrong horse in most of the wars of liberation and civil wars in Southern Africa, British troops are not exactly flavour of the month anywhere in the region at the moment, so the whole operation must be covert from start to finish. It's a deniable op in hostile territory so all the kit you wear and use must not be identifiable as British and you should either travel to the op as civilians, using a solid cover story to explain your presence, or make a covert insertion.'

'Do you know what, Jonathan?' Shepherd said. 'We're big boys, with a lot of experience in this line of work, so why don't you leave the hows and whens to us, and just concentrate on the whats and wheres?'

Parker's smile grew even more forced. 'I'm just giving you the background, but obviously the tactics are entirely up to you. The hostage was taken from a lodge at Victoria Falls in Zimbabwe, but we've good intel to suggest they have crossed into Namibia and are now in a hideout in the Caprivi Strip. A little history may help here. In 1890 Britain and Germany tried to tidy up their colonial possessions and avoid future disputes over their African territories by arranging a swap. Britain gave up Heligoland in the North Sea in exchange for the Germans abandoning all claims to Zanzibar and recognising Britain's East Coast colonies. To sweeten the deal with the

Germans, HMG also threw in what became known as the Caprivi Strip. It had been the northernmost part of Bechuanaland - now called Botswana - and was 280 miles long but only as little as twenty miles wide, running pretty much due East from the north of the German colony of South West Africa, that is now Namibia. In the apartheid era, South Africa tried and failed to make the Caprivi Strip a segregated Bantustan, a dumping ground for unwanted African tribes, in other words. But then during the "Bush Wars" from the mid-1960s onwards - that's the African bush, not George Bush,' he said with heavy sarcasm-'

'Try not to be too patronising, Jonathan,' Shepherd said, before Parker could finish his sentence. 'I know that in most regiments of the British Army if you've got a GCSE in Woodwork you're liable to be nicknamed "Brains", but while we SAS men don't tend to have much in the way of academic qualifications, we're not without intelligence and we do tend to be fairly well informed about history and politics. That's mainly because if we're being asked to risk our lives - as we so often are - then as a general principle, we like to know why. So I and I'm sure, most of my comrades, have actually heard of the Bush Wars and the Caprivi Strip.'

Parker shrugged. 'So you'll also know that this Namibian salient is the place where four other countries meet or come within touching distance: Zimbabwe, Zambia, Angola and Botswana. The porous borders between them all made the Caprivi Strip notorious in those Bush Wars. That period saw continual infiltration and fighting by all sides and, despite the alleged end of hostilities, it's still going on there now. When the kidnappers seized their hostage, they took out all the lodge's CCTV cameras on their way in - or at least they must have thought they had. In fact there was a camera fixed to a tree trunk overlooking the car park which they missed. We've obtained the footage from that and it shows them entering the car park in two Toyota Land Cruisers - one of which had what appears to be a .50 Browning machine gun mounted on the rear - and then leaving again a few minutes later, bundling their hostage into one of the Land Cruisers before driving off. She was bound and gagged but otherwise appeared to be unharmed at that stage. That CCTV footage also revealed that the kidnappers are not, as we at first suspected, either a criminal gang or black Africans from one of the losing factions in the Bush Wars. In fact they are white, and intercepted comms, courtesy of GCHQ, plus the kidnappers' demands that have now been received at the US Embassy in Pretoria, show they are unreconstructed white supremacist backwoodsmen. And they are not just Yarpies' he said, using the derogatory term for Boers derived from the Afrikaner word for farm boy. 'There are also British, Portuguese and Belgian ex-colonials, all no doubt still bitter and resentful at the "betrayal" that has handed their former territories to black nationalists. They are determined to carve a new white homeland - a *Volkstaat*, as they call it - out of parts of Namibia and the Northern Cape province of South Africa which, though nowhere near a majority of the population, has the highest proportion of white residents in the country - most of them Afrikaners - and of "Cape coloureds": mixed race inhabitants. The whites see their hostage as a bargaining chip to achieve, if not American support, at least tacit American acquiescence in those plans, with some accompanying arm-twisting in Pretoria and Windhoek to make it happen. It's a delusion of course, it's never going to happen, but to make sure the hostage is kept alive, the Yanks are playing along with negotiations for the moment. Now there are no CCTV cameras in the bush, of course, so there is no other footage of them, but we were able to heighten the resolution from the car park camera enough to get a partial identification of the registration plate of one of the Land Cruisers. Our second bit of luck is that the Caprivi Strip is bubbling up into a potential civil war with a group called the Caprivi Liberation Front agitating for independence from Namibia. So the cousins had positioned a geostationary satellite over the Strip, just in case the Russians or Chinese decide to take a hand, and that has given us a real breakthrough, because imagery from that satellite has allowed us to track the kidnappers to the compound where they are currently holed up with their hostage. The problem for us with this location is, as

I've just indicated, that while it is in Namibian territory, it is very close to the borders of four other countries, so if they receive any advance warning of an
attempt to free the hostage or even if they decide to
change locations for some other reason, it may well
be necessary to cross one or more of those frontiers
in pursuit of them.' He shrugged. 'Which is fine of
course, but if any or all of a rescue force were appre-
hended by that country's authorities, either while
crossing the border or further inside their territory,
then HMG would be forced to deny any knowledge
of, or responsibility for you.'

'So what else is new?' Shepherd said. 'That's
pretty much a given in all our ops.'

'Just so,' Parker said. 'Now just to add a further
cautionary note, these particular Yarpies have been
terrorising the native populations in the areas where
they operate, and so too have the Namibian paramilitaries, the SFF - the Special Field Force. They were
created three years ago by the appropriately named
Namibian police commissioner Ruben "Danger"
Ashipala, as an aggressive auxiliary unit to operate
alongside the Special Reserve Force, but the SFF is
widely seen by the civilian population - not without
considerable justification - as a brutal force simply
tasked with cowing and intimidating them. It has
carried out a series of assaults, acts of torture and
murders of civilians suspected of being supporters or
sympathisers with the Caprivi Liberation Front, and
several thousand civilians have become refugees in

makeshift camps across the border with Botswana. So as well as those white supremacist kidnappers, there is no shortage whatsoever of other armed gangs roaming the Caprivi Strip and that will all have to be factored into your planning for the op.'

'So I've got all the context,' Shepherd said, anxious to cut to the chase, 'but who is the hostage?'

'She's what makes this very political for the cousins,' Parker said, using the standard euphemism for the Americans. 'The girl who's been abducted is Kesia Keita, the daughter of a US congressman. If it becomes publicly known that he'd not only brought his daughter along on an official overseas trip but then allowed her to fall into hostile hands, then he will be under considerable political pressure at home, hence the preference for a covert, deniable mission to rescue her. Also they don't altogether trust their own special forces to do the job - as you know, there have been more than enough cock-ups by them in the recent to make even the most patriotic American wary of entrusting another sensitive op to them - so they've appealed to us through the usual channels to make the SAS available. The Congressman is seen as a coming man in US politics, so we're hoping to create a debt of gratitude and/or obligation that Britain will be able to draw down against in the future.'

'To be honest I don't want the bloody job and I have been trying to think of a way of tactfully declining it without ruffling too many feathers,' said the CO archly.

'Or damaging your future promotion prospects,' Shepherd thought to himself. 'Tell you what, Boss,' Shepherd said to his CO, ignoring Parker. 'Let's not reject the idea out of hand. Give me a couple of hours and I'll see if I can put together a team to do the job. There's no problem in using Taffy to take me down to Stirling Lines is there?'

'Be my guest,' the CO said. 'But I'm telling you we're down to the bare bones, so I'm not sure what sort of team you'll actually be able to assemble.'

CHAPTER 8

'Where now? The Saracen's Head?' Taffy said hopefully, as Shepherd got back in the car.

'Sorry no, mate, I'll have to save that pleasure for another time. Go straight to camp would you, and put the pedal to the metal.'

'Is there any other way to drive?' Taffy said, gunning it towards the gates.

Stirling Lines was normally so bulging at the seams that plans were already well advanced to move the Regiment to a new and much more capacious base a few miles outside Hereford. However, as the CO had already indicated to Shepherd, for once it was almost completely deserted. The members of the Counter-Terrorist Wing were all out at the PATA, carrying out the endless training regimes to sharpen and heighten their formidable skills still further while they waited on stand-by for the call to arms that rarely came, but to which they always had to be ready to respond at a moment's notice. The rest of the active service troops - the Revolutionary Warfare Wing (the squadron set up to carry out plain clothes, deniable ops around the world) and the other Sabre squadrons - were all away on ops. As a result, none of the members of his usual patrol - the hard-nosed, fiery-tempered Glaswegian, Jock, the lanky signaller, Jimbo, or the wise-cracking patrol medic, Geordie - were available.

Shepherd obtained a list of the active service troops who were still in Hereford and available for an op from the duty sergeant manning the office. He scanned down the list and rejected a few names out of hand. One was a blowhard, who could talk the talk but had never really walked the walk, though you would have struggled to realise that from the tune he tooted on his own trumpet. Another two were veterans of undisputed skill and courage but, although still young in terms of the general population, they were getting on in years for active service, and Shepherd was also concerned that they might both have been suffering from battle fatigue. SAS men tended to give short shrift to any reference to PTSD, but Shepherd was a firm subscriber to the belief that you could only go to the well of courage so often. Once you reached your own personal limit - and that might happen out of the blue, at any time, with no advance warning, then even the bravest man might find he no longer had it in him to go into battle.

He rejected another trooper purely on the basis of personal dislike. There was no objective reason he could find for it, but in the close confines and under the high tension and pressure of an active service op, any grievance could rapidly flare up into a situation that could jeopardise the op. He dismissed a few more men for a variety of reasons, but it still took him no more than half an hour to assemble a viable patrol.

His first recruit was Joe Levula, a Fijian who had been serving with the Regiment for ten years and had missed out on deploying overseas with the rest of his squadron this time because he was still recovering from one of his recurring bouts of malaria. It was a bit of a cruel irony for a man who was a patrol medic. Normally contracting malaria was an RTU offence - Returned To Unit, sacked from the Regiment - for SAS men because it was a preventible disease. If you kept your sleeves rolled down and buttoned, wore long trousers and smothered all exposed skin in Deet insect repellent, you wouldn't get bitten by mosquitoes and so wouldn't contract the disease. However, Joe was exempted from that because he had originally contracted malaria when he was a kid, long before he had enlisted in the army and later joined the SAS. His malaria still flared up from time to time, putting him flat on his back until the fever passed, but it had now left him again and, bored stiff with sitting round the almost deserted camp, he jumped at the chance to join Shepherd's op. 'You sure you're over the malaria?' Shepherd said.

'I'm sure, until the next bout anyway,' said Joe. 'But it's usually at least a couple of years before it flares up again, so you don't need to have any worries on that account.' Shepherd had no other doubts about him because though they had not worked together before, he'd heard enough about him from chatting to his mates to know that he was a doughty fighter and a brilliant battlefield medic.

The next patrol member was another Fijian, Sam Vakatoa, who was due to go on Inter-Tour Leave - a period of home leave that normally took precedence over anything else, even a deployment - but who was more than happy to postpone that for a potential taste of action. He was three or four inches shorter than Shepherd but he had a barrel chest and a neck that you could have bent a steel bar around. He could carry a fully-laden Bergen up a mountain as if it weighed no more than a backpack with a few sandwiches and bags of crisps in it, and if it came to unarmed combat he was in a league of his own.

The third member of the patrol Shepherd recruited was a South African of English descent, a linguist christened James "Jimmy" Rhodes, but universally known around the Regiment as "Mr Angry", because although he was a bloody good soldier, he was also a ticking time-bomb with a very short fuse. He had been busted down to private and was due to be RTUed after an argument with a fellow corporal with whom he had a long standing, bitter grievance that had escalated into a fight that had put the other man in hospital with a broken nose and a fractured eye socket. However only the CO could order an RTU and since he was closeted in the War Bunker for the duration of the overseas op, Mr Angry remained at Stirling Lines. Shepherd knew him of old and was confident he could handle Mr Angry's fiery temperament and make use of his skill-set, his experience of soldiering in the African bush and his ability to speak the local Xhosa and Shona languages.

Having assembled his team, he gave them brief details of the op they were going to be carrying out. 'As you know, on a covert op, we'd normally be going in on a commercial flight, in civilian clothes and with a plausible cover story. However, in this case, there is a considerable need for speed - we're tasked with rescuing a girl who's been kidnapped - and the site where she's being held is a very long way from any commercial airport, so we're going to insert using an Ultra Low Level drop.'

Mr Angry scowled. 'A ULL drop? Using an untested technique is adding a pretty high level of risk, isn't it? We'll not be much use to the girl if we're all lying out in the bush nursing broken ankles.'

'It was untested,' Shepherd said, 'but I've just been working on the technique at Fort Benning, and I'm confident I've got all the bugs out of the system; as you can see, neither of my ankles is broken. So are we all happy to go with it?'

'Sure,' Joe said. 'Better than hanging around in the air for half an hour, waiting for the bloody chute to open.'

Leaving them to sort out their kit and transfer to the training area, Shepherd got Taffy to make another high speed run back to the PATA. As he dropped him off, Shepherd gave him another job. 'We're going on a deniable op, Taffy. So we need clothing that can't be traced back to the UK military. Can you do a fast run to that outdoor superstore in Cheltenham and load up with generic gear? Get half a dozen of everything and don't worry too much about sizes - a mix of medium and large should fit everyone near enough.' He paused. 'Hang on, better add one set of XXLs to the mix. Sam Vakatoa will be bursting out of anything smaller.'

Contrary to what their tabloid image might have led people to believe, with the exception of Sam Vakatoa, SAS men were not muscle-bound XXL giants. There were no fitter soldiers anywhere in the world, and they could force march for huge distances carrying Bergens so heavy that most people would have struggled to pick them up, let alone trek over mountains, deserts or through jungle with them. Yet most SAS men were of medium build, iron-muscled but often whippet thin.

While Taffy drove off, Shepherd went to report to the CO in the War Bunker. To his relief, he found that Parker had already departed.

'Okay Boss,' Shepherd said. 'I've managed to put together a quality patrol and if you give us the go-ahead, we can sort everything out. Like you said, a joint op with Delta is not on, but if we lead and they provide support, it'll give them the result they want.

And they know that if they try to go it alone they'll be risking another Eagle Claw fiasco.'

The CO nodded. Nobody in the US military needed any reminding about the disastrous attempt to rescue American hostages from Iran in 1980 after the Shah had been deposed and the Ayatollahs had taken over. It was a symmetrical end to the Shah's reign since he owed his throne to an American-backed coup that had deposed the previous regime. The Eagle Claw operation was a shambles from start to finish, no hostages were rescued, eight American servicemen lost their lives and a transport aircraft and six helicopters were either destroyed or left behind when the surviving American troops were pulled out. Ironically the operation had been led by Charlie Beckwith, a Delta Force officer who had served on an exchange with the SAS and returned to Fort Bragg determined to transform US Special Forces into an American replica of the SAS. He had failed and as he later privately conceded in conversations with his British comrades, the op had been doomed from the start, mainly because there were simply too many different US agencies involved in it and far too much complex kit.

The op could have and should have been done successfully, and, if given the task, the SAS would have carried it out following their traditional KISS motto - Keep It Simple Stupid - and gone in with a straightforward plan and just enough kit to do the job, with a high probability of success. By contrast, the plan the US Special Forces were saddled with was far too complex, the men carrying it out were almost buried under the weight of high tech kit and equipment they were issued with, and the inevitable result was that instead of success, it became a disaster and a national humiliation. The fiasco not only killed President Carter's chances of being re-elected but it made his successors very wary of further military adventures unless they were certain that their troops had an overwhelming advantage that would guarantee success. So the near-farcical invasion by massed US forces of the tiny Caribbean island of Grenada went ahead under Ronald Reagan, but the Gulf War was only launched under President Bush once a massive multi-national coalition of allied forces had been assembled, and once the Saudis had agreed to underwrite almost the entire cost of it.

The CO thought about it for a few more seconds and then gave his approval. However, before the op could proceed, it needed a formal, high level authorisation, known as an Operations Order. There were two ways to achieve it, the diplomatic route or the military route. Using the diplomatic route, the request went from SAS Group HQ in London via 10 Downing Street and the British Embassy in Washington to the White House, sidestepping all the usual diplomatic channels. The military route went from SAS group HQ via the MoD and the Chief of Staff, to the Pentagon, the US Joint Chiefs of Staff and the White House. Once Presidential approval had been secured, if Shepherd wanted anything, even a satellite, he would get one with no questions asked, and the usual 'Who pays?' question that could often bedevil joint ops would be easily answered.

Shepherd and the CO also had to assign a security classification to the op. The highest grade was Above Top Secret but if you made it too high then literally no one could talk about it, so the working classification was the standard Top Secret. Everything was on a need to know basis - if you didn't, you weren't told - but the team carrying out the op could discuss it freely among themselves with only minor restrictions. In this op, for example, the real name of the hostage would never be used. She would be known as Belle and those holding her would simply be identified as Bandit 1, 2, 3 and so on.

In a hostage situation, everyone knew that speed was vital and the request was moved up the chain and approved in record time, and within four hours Shepherd had also drawn up and passed on his list of requests. The CO at Fort Benning received an order to deploy a C141 to RAF Lakenheath in Suffolk diverting to Fort Bragg en route in order to pick up an Intelligence Officer and a Comms specialist from Delta Force. It would already be carrying an air and ground crew, and the specialist parachute rigger, Lula, with ten chutes. Her orders were that she was being assigned to "TDY" - the American acronym for Temporary Duty - for an unspecified length of time.

Within a very short time, the aircraft was rumbling down the runway at Fort Bragg and taking off on its long flight. When it landed at Lakenheath - it was badged as an RAF establishment but most of the aircraft, personnel and equipment were American - an RAF Puma was already waiting, its rotors idly turning, and Lula and the two Delta force operatives were at once transferred to it and flown down to the PATA. The captain of the C141 was meanwhile briefed to refuel and keep himself and his crew in readiness to fly to Southern Africa at two hours' notice.

Shepherd and his patrol members had already gone into isolation at the PATA with their three-man support team: Intelligence and Comms specialists and Taffy as their driver and gofer. Shepherd and the patrol began talking through the op, testing and challenging each other's ideas, and modifying their plan constantly until they had what they all felt was a workable solution. They obtained all the kit, weapons, ammo and explosives they might need and called up all the available intelligence.

The Int Officer's briefing included a psychological profile that had been put together on the hostage. 'It's a cause for concern,' he said, 'because it identifies her as fragile and vulnerable but also very headstrong. We won't ever know if those traits contributed to her being kidnapped, because her security team are both dead and can't tell us, but the Secret Service agent who was with her had previously reported that on three occasions, she had ignored instructions and put herself in potential jeopardy. She's also a strong feminist - nothing wrong with that, except that it may make her less inclined to take orders from macho men like you guys.'

Shepherd gave a rueful smile. 'That's one problem I hadn't anticipated.' He thought for a few moments. 'We may need help with this. Keep working on the plan, I'm going to talk to the MO.'

As Shepherd hurried out, Sam Vakatoa gave the others a puzzled look. 'What's the Medical Officer got to do with it?'

'Beats me,' Mr Angry said. 'She's a woman, but that's all I know about her. Like the rest of you guys, if I've got a health problem, my first port of call is the patrol medic, not the camp MO.'

Taffy had once more tested the speed limits on the run back into Hereford and within twenty minutes Shepherd was talking to the MO. Helen Williams was a redhead with grey-green eyes and skin so pale it was the colour of skimmed milk. She had been posted to the Regiment the previous year. Feisty, very ambitious and with a powerful self-belief, she had qualified as a doctor, then gone through Sandhurst and served with the Paras before wangling a posting to the SAS because she thought it was the best way to get ahead. However, to her disappointment and then mounting fury, she found that she was given no training or active involvement role with the Regiment, and instead was basically working as a GP on a military base. Even more frustratingly, she rarely had any dealings with the men of the Sabre Squadrons - the fighting troops. If any of them had a medical problem, like Mr Angry, their first thought was always to consult the patrol medic, so the only patients she saw were the officers and others on attachment to the SAS. So when Shepherd turned up to see her and began outlining his concerns about the hostage, she interrupted him at once. 'I'll go with you,' she said. 'I can take charge of her and if necessary I can use the liquid cosh to keep her under control.' She saw his dubious expression. 'You don't need to worry about me. I'm infantry- and Para-trained. I've got the skills.'

Shepherd nodded. 'But a covert op in very hostile territory is very different from any training exercise, no matter how realistic.'

'I don't care. All I've been doing here is sitting on my arse. If I go with you, I promise you I'll be an asset, not a liability.'

Eventually, almost despite himself, Shepherd was convinced. 'Okay, but if you go, it is purely to look after the girl,' he said. 'The rest of us have the patrol medic.' He smiled as he saw her hackles rising. 'I'm sure you could teach him a lot but there's a hell of a lot you could learn from him too. We see ten times more active service ops and combat than other units, so he's had more experience of dealing with battle-field trauma than any Army doctor and his knowledge of primitive medicine is astonishing too.'

She nodded. 'Okay. I hear you.'

'Terrific. Welcome aboard. Now you've got thirty minutes to arrange cover for your absence. Don't worry about bringing any personal kit, since this is a deniable op, nothing can be traceable back to the UK, let alone the UK military, so all our clothes and other kit will be coming from a generic outdoor store, selling gear that could have come from anywhere in the world. It might even be ex-Soviet, so don't expect comfort or a good fit. However looking at that skin of yours, something you will definitely be needing to sort out is a shedload of fake tan and heavy duty sun-block. At the moment your skin is so white you could probably be seen from space but after a few hours under the African sun, if you don't protect yourself, I'm guessing you'll be turning pillar box red.'

'Don't worry,' she said. 'I'll take a bush hat.'

He grinned. 'Oh, and by the way, as I'm sure you know, we don't use our real names on ops, so from now on, you'll be known simply as Doc, and my handle is Spider.'

'Spider? Really?'

He nodded. 'I ate a tarantula on a training exercise in the jungle.' He clocked her expression. 'It was no big deal.' Shepherd glanced at his watch. 'So, you've got half an hour tops and then I need to get you on the range out at the PATA and show you how to fire a nine mil semi-automatic.'

Her hackles went back up. 'I know how to do that, I fired hundreds of rounds in training with the Paras.'

'No doubt, but the Army way is not the SAS way. We do things differently.'

She was back with her kit inside twenty minutes and Taffy drove them back out to the PATA, where Shepherd took her straight out to the range. He handed her a 9mm semi-automatic and watched with approval as she checked it, stripped down, put it back together and loaded the magazine with another round up the spout. 'Okay,' he said, positioning her in front of a close-range target. 'I'm telling you this purely so you can save your own life if it comes to it. You can forget everything you've been taught about shooting in the past. So you're not aiming at anything, you're just pointing out something to someone, like you would if you were showing one of your relatives the sights of Hereford - not that that would take long,' he added with a wink. 'There it is, right over there,' he said, indicating the target. 'So point to it with the hand holding the pistol and just let your gaze track it. Keep your eyes open.'

She took aim. No, forget about the iron sights,' he said, as he saw her trying to aim along the barrel. 'Just look at where you want the round to hit. Now you have to wait until the target is close enough to touch and when he is squeeze the trigger. Don't worry about fancy stuff like double taps or any of that, just pull the trigger and at that range, that's all you'll need to do.'

He watched her as she practised, firing off half a dozen magazines, and then pronounced himself satisfied. 'You'll do, Doc,' he said. 'Okay, time to come and meet the rest of the team.'

Back in the bunker, having made the introductions, Shepherd resumed leading the whole team through the pre-op briefing. He had also asked a couple of guys from the Counter Terrorist team to be present to give him an oversight - quality control, in case Shepherd and his team missed any potential flaws in their plan. That had never been done until the aftermath of the disastrous eight-man Bravo Two Zero patrol into Iraq during the Gulf War, which led to the death of three patrol members and the capture of four others, including the patrol leader. While popular mythology, fed by the accounts published by several of the survivors, had turned Bravo Two Zero into another Dunkirk-style victory out of defeat narrative, members of the Regiment took a much less rose-coloured view of the operation and the errors that had led to its embarrassing failure. The lessons had been learned and oversight by non-members of the operational team was now routine in the planning stage of all SAS operations.

'Okay,' Shepherd said. 'The first question to be answered on any op is "Who's the boss?" And just in case you're in any doubt about this one, the answer is "You're looking at him". This is the forum to raise questions and express doubts, if any. Once we're in theatre, I don't ever want to hear a disagreement or dispute about the plan, and if anything goes wrong, nor do I ever want to hear anyone afterwards saying

"I thought it was a bad idea". If you thought that, you should have said so in the planning phase. If you didn't, then you've given up all right to complain afterwards. Clear?'

There were nods of agreement from around the room. 'Right. As I told you we'll be inserting by a ULL drop,' Shepherd continued. 'Bergens will be dropped separately but only using ten foot drogue chutes, so best not to pack the Waterford crystal, and the weaponry we'll be using will be the MP5K because we can strap those to our chests, using a combat string, and fixing them under our parachute harnesses so they don't fly up in the slipstream and knock our teeth out. We won't be able to access them during the descent, obviously, so if we come under fire, we'll also have a 9mm semi-automatic strapped to our leg. And we'll carry an aircrew rescue knife on the other leg so if your jump ends with you fifty feet up in an acacia tree, you'll be able to cut yourself free.'

He looked around and everyone was nodding. So far so good. 'We are also going to need to carry slings for our MP5s as well.' Shepherd saw Mr Angry and the two Fijians exchange dubious looks. Weapon slings were never normally used in the SAS because on active service ops weapons were always carried in the hands at all times, ready to be used. The delay of even a second or so involved in unslinging your weapon from your chest or shoulder and bringing it to bear could easily be the difference between life and death. 'I know, we wouldn't normally dream of using slings,' Shepherd said, 'but the one time where they do confer an advantage is when we're assaulting a building. We've been tasked with the rescue of a hostage currently located somewhere inside a building at the centre of the target compound. In order to effect that rescue, we may be diving through doors or windows to clear rooms of hostiles, and then handling a hostage who may well be injured or hysterical and difficult to control, so it's well worth carrying a sling to be able to have our hands free in those situations.'

He gave a rueful smile. 'Of course you won't find a weapon sling for love or money anywhere in Hereford, so as usual, we're going to have to improvise. And like we always say, there's nothing that man's ingenuity can devise that we can't replicate using para cord and gaffer tape.'

'We'll need at least one full calibre weapon as well,' Mr Angry said, 'something with a bit of thump. We're going to be operating in sub-tropical Africa and in case anyone hadn't noticed, there are a shitload of wild animals down there.'

Joe nodded. 'I can carry an SLR with a folding stock. That 7.62 Nato round will knock an elephant down.'

'I hear you,' Shepherd said. The 7.62 had about six times the range of the MP5 and pretty much six times the punch as well but, as he warned Joe, 'It's too big a weapon to carry on a ULL jump.'

'I'll strap it down my right side,' Joe said. 'It'll be fine.'

Shepherd gave him a dubious look. 'We've no time to practise this.'

Joe shrugged. 'Trust me, Spider. It'll be okay. I'm a big boy.'

'All right. Now we'll use the MP5s without optical sights. Opticals will just move around or get broken and we'll have to dump them anyway so we'll just go with the iron sights. We'll take night vision goggles but they're likely to suffer the same issues so we'll base our plan on not having them available. We'll also be taking some flash bangs. Smoke only ones would probably do the job, but we'll take a couple of CS gas ones as well just in case of unforeseen problems.'

SAS patrols had access to three different kinds of flash bangs that they could use on ops: CR gas, CS gas and smoke only. CR flash bangs used a gas - dibenzoxozepine - that had been developed as a riot control agent by the chemical and biological weapons establishment at Porton Down, and they could only be used by troops equipped with respirators. CR gas was ten times more powerful than CS gas, so toxic that it caused temporary blindness and such severe breathing difficulties that it was given the nickname "Firegas".

Flash bangs contained scores of tiny "cassettes" which scattered as the stun grenade went off, filling the air and the ground with mini-projectiles that all pumped out smoke, ensuring instant, blanket smoke coverage, with no gaps or eddies in the smoke that could expose an attacker to hostile fire. They also had an instant fuse; when they were thrown they detonated immediately, whereas conventional explosive grenades had a three to five second delay built in to allow the thrower to take cover and or lob the grenade far enough to put himself safely out of range of the resulting blast and shrapnel. Whereas standard explosive grenades had a short, one inch detonator, flash bangs had a detonator that ran the entire length of the grenade. That meant that in addition to being detonated by pulling the pin, a flash bang could also be set off when it was hit by a round anywhere along its length. That might put a trooper carrying one at a small additional risk if he came under enemy fire, but it also meant that an SAS man could place or roll a flash bang into position without pulling the pin and then detonate it subsequently by firing a round from his rifle into it.

'We'll also be needing four standard charges,' Shepherd said, 'and the necessary initiation sets - both electrical ones and, in case of problems with them, old school safety fuses. The detonators are a bit sensitive so I'll jump with them and, if I get through the drop OK, I'll distribute them around the rest of the patrol at the Drop Zone RV.'

The standard charge contained one and a half pounds of PE - plastic explosive - and, until the initiation set was fitted, it was so inert that it could be carried on the body and even dropped or kicked without the slightest risk of it exploding; PE could even be used as fuel for a fire without the faintest danger of it detonating. When confined within a standard charge and fitted with an ignition set, however, it became a lethal explosive, capable of demolishing a building and killing everyone within it.

'Comms are pretty straightforward,' Shepherd said. 'When we're in theatre we're going to be on our own, so there'll be nothing coming our way except a Go or No Go check every twelve hours. "Knife and Fork" will mean "Go", "Empty Plate" means "Abort". And there'll be no comms going back to base from us either, except a burst transmission to call in a Herc to the Landing Zone to come and lift us out after the job's done.'

A burst transmission was just like sending an email. The signaller wrote the message first and then sent it in a burst lasting a millisecond, greatly reducing the chances of it being intercepted. Even if anyone was monitoring the frequency, all they would hear would be a beep. If it was intercepted, the message was also encrypted so unless the enemy had their own genius cypher clerks, it was unlikely to be decoded soon enough for the information it contained to be of any use to them.

SAS communications as a whole were as sophisticated and secure as technology could make them. Most operational comms were carried out over satphones and were auto-encrypted. If even greater security was needed they were sent using a one-time pad and five figure groups, so even though the communication was in voice, it would transmit in code. As a further safeguard, outgoing comms were transmitted from the PATA but incoming ones were received at Stirling Lines in Hereford, avoiding possible conflicts and messages becoming scrambled.

At patrol level, codes only had to be secure enough to last twenty-four hours, because by then the patrol would have moved anyway and the information would be useless to anyone intercepting it, but at squadron level the codes were designed to be secure for much longer. The Regiment was so meticulous about the security of its messages that when coded messages had to be sent to GCHQ in Cheltenham to be decrypted, the SAS would often send a helicopter to pick up a hard copy, rather than risk having a message being intercepted between GCHQ and Stirling Lines.

CHAPTER 9

The patrol's briefing was interrupted by the arrival of the Americans and Shepherd broke off to brief Lula. 'I need you to go to the RAF centre at the Camp,' he said. 'There are a couple of riggers there who normally modify and pack our chutes for us. I want you to take those ten chutes you've brought with you, show them how to modify them in exactly the same way you did for me, and supervise them closely to make sure they do it right.'

As Lula was whisked off to carry out her task, Shepherd returned to the briefing with the American Intelligence Officer and the Comms specialist. Although they were attached to Delta Force, they were not fighting troops but part of Delta's support network. The Intelligence Officer was in PATA to give the SAS team access to the most up to date mapping and intelligence information from the US agencies, including the NSA - the American equivalent of GCHQ. Britain had no direct access to intel like satellite surveillance over Southern Africa and was reliant on American cooperation to provide it.

The Communications Officer's role was both to provide information out of the latest intercepted comms
from Southern Africa and to set up communications
between the PATA and Fort Benning, Fort Bragg,
SOCOM and the US Air Force, bypassing the usual
channels that could slow the flow of comms down to
a crawl.

The Int Officer, Kent "Stonewall" Jackson, looked
and sounded like a Southern "good ol' boy" with a
slow drawl of an accent, blue eyes and straw-coloured
hair. 'Stonewall's quite a handle,' Shepherd said,
after introducing him to the rest of the team. 'Is that
because you're as hard as one, or something else?'

Jackson laughed. 'It sure as hell wasn't that. It
came courtesy of my Daddy. When I was growing
up, we didn't exactly see eye to eye on a lot of things
because he was a real old school Southerner - and
that's the polite way of putting it. The Civil War had
never ended for him. He flew the Confederate flag
from the flagpole at the end of the stoop outside
our house and I reckon if you'd cut him open, you'd
have found "The South will rise again" engraved on
his heart. He chose Stonewall as my middle name in
tribute to his hero, General Stonewall Jackson. My
mom had no say in it. She was still in hospital when
Daddy went down to register the birth. She said she
nearly gave birth again when he admitted what he'd
done.' He grinned. 'He died a few years back and I
reckon he'd have been spinning in his grave when
the Stonewall riots broke out. I took a whole mess of

barracking at work over that, I can tell you. Anyways, I enlisted mainly to please him, I guess and though I did like a lot about the army, apart from the bull, marching and parades, when there was a chance to get into Intelligence work, I grabbed it with both hands and never looked back. And I'm a big admirer of you guys in the SAS, so it's good to be working with you, right Zig?'

The comms specialist nodded. 'Sure is. Name's Zig, short for Zbigniew - and even I can't pronounce that.'

Shepherd smiled politely at what was obviously a well worn joke. Zig was more powerfully built than any comms specialist that Shepherd had previously met, with a wedge-shaped upper body that spoke of long hours pumping iron in the gym, but he had an open, friendly face beneath his fringe of brown hair.

Introductions complete, Shepherd handed over to the Americans. 'Okay gents, you're up.'

'Right,' Jackson said, speaking for both of them. 'The compound where the hostage is being held was used by white mercenaries, and by South African and South West African paramilitaries, and Rhodesian special forces during the Bush Wars but it had been lying abandoned and derelict for the last ten years until these Yarpies decided to base themselves in it. There is also a training area about half a mile away with a dozen six-man tents alongside it. Our surveillance imagery shows that some if not all of them are occupied, so clearly a decision is needed on whether

the hostage can be extracted fast enough to prevent them from joining the fight. The compound
itself covers about an acre. There are three buildings within it, an ablutions block and an accommodation block, both built against the perimeter wall
and a separate single-storey building in the centre
of the compound where we believe the hostage is
being held. We have satellite imagery, including one
image that shows a young black woman, dressed in
Western clothes and closely resembling the hostage,
Belle, being escorted by two of the Yarpies across the
compound to the ablutions block. We also have good
imagery of the surrounding terrain. It's a mixture
of savannah, bush, forest, marsh and wetlands with
several large rivers, including the Okavango, Chobe,
Cubango and, last but not least, the Zambezi. In the
wet season, which is just coming to an end, they are
all liable to flood. It looks likely that you will have to
make a river crossing to reach the site covertly, and it
may well be in spate when you do so; you will need to
build that into your planning and kit list. The dense
forests and wetland vegetation, especially reeds,
makes for slow progress away from the roads and
almost all of them are unimproved tracks - dustbowls
in the dry season and swamps in the wet. The Caprivi
Strip is also a malarial zone, and there are the usual
range of other unpleasant African diseases including
dengue fever and bilharzia - river blindness - to worry
about, so make sure all your shots are up to date.
It's a sparsely populated land, most people living in

small villages and dependent on subsidence agricul-
ture augmented by fishing and hunting. Bands of
San - bushmen - operate in the far west but you're
unlikely to encounter any of them where you're heading, though if things go wrong and you have to exfil
in that direction, the *San* have the local knowledge
to keep you alive, even in the heart of the desert.' He
gave a cynical smile. 'So try not to piss them off, if
you come across any.'

He handed over to the British Intelligence officer to finish the next part of the briefing. 'Right, a
word of warning: do not for a moment underestimate
the fighting qualities of the enemy. They may sound
like a bunch of the sort of angry, middle-aged white
men you might meet down at the British Legion or
the local Masonic Lodge, but we suspect that most,
if not all of them fought with the SADF - the South
African Defence Forces - or the Rhodesian Light
Infantry or as paramilitaries or mercenaries during the Bush Wars. Some mercenaries may be Serbs,
former members of the "White Legion" that fought
for a while in Zaire and there may even still be some
American veterans of Vietnam, so it is possible that
there are American citizens among the kidnappers.
However we'll leave the Yanks to deal with any political fall-out from that, our job is to neutralise all the
kidnappers, irrespective of their nationalities. Most
of them are probably veterans of counter-insurgency
units like the South African *Koevoet* and 32 Battalion,
the Rhodesian Selous Scouts, or the Portuguese

Flechas who operated in Angola and Mozambique. It doesn't really matter which of those you encounter, because they were all notorious for summary executions and atrocities against suspected insurgents and their families. So they are battle-hardened and they are also extremely well-armed, having liberated huge caches of weaponry prior to the handover to the ANC in South Africa, SWAPO in Namibia and ZANU in Zimbabwe. Oh, and one last piece of intel: there are several gangs of African poachers accompanied by Chinese nationals in the area where you're operating, killing and capturing game for food and traditional medicine. It's not part of our brief to deal with poaching, of course, but as well as the possibility of encountering rebels from the Caprivi Liberation Army, the poaching gangs represent an additional potential threat that may have to be dealt with.'

'Okay,' Shepherd said. 'And keep in mind that those Bush Wars also left the border areas of all the southern African countries - Namibia, South Africa, Zimbabwe, Zambia, Botswana, Angola and Mozambique - littered with landmines. Very few of them have been cleared. When we're infiltrating our target, as well as angry hippos, rhinos, elephants and lions, we need to be alert to the danger of mines. So, based on that intel, the first decision we have to make is whether, as well as taking out the forces in the compound, we also need to be eliminating the ones who are based at the training area. They're only in soft-skinned shelters - tents - but since the surveillance shows a dozen six-man tents, to take that lot out would involve a whole different order of difficulty and a lot more fire-power than our small patrol can muster on its own.' He smiled. 'We may be SAS but, despite what the Sun newspaper might want its readers to believe, we're not superheroes. So to get rid of the forces at the training area we'd have to be talking heli or fixed wing gunships with Hellfire missiles and rotary cannon, plus a platoon of ground troops - the whole nine yards in fact - and while that shit-show is going on, the hostage is going to be at great risk of either being killed or moved to another location. So I'd suggest our best option is to forget about the training area, focus on the compound and plan to be in and out fast enough to prevent the other forces having time to react. Anyone disagree?'

Nobody spoke. There were several nods and no dissent.

'Okay,' said Shepherd. 'Now we're going to be operating on hard routine. That means dry rations and no cooking or lights. You can take whatever rations you like but they've got to be high calorie, light weight and not needing water to reconstitute them, so something like high energy bars will be the way to go. Next: mapping. Courtesy of our friends here,' he nodded towards Jackson and Zig, 'We have sat pix of the DZ, LZ and the target - the compound where the girl is being held, on the edge of the Caprivi Strip.'

He glanced at Doc. 'This isn't common knowledge outside the Regiment, but we have a computer system that can convert satellite imagery into a plan view. It turns it into a map in other words, complete with grid squares, contour lines, the works. So we finish up with something that looks like an OS map but is as up to date as the satellite photo it was taken from, just minutes old in other words. We can not only use it to navigate to the target but to plot the possible locations of sentries and to create a site plan of the target. Using mine tape - the stuff they use to demarcate minefields - we can physically create the outline of the target compound and buildings on the ground, to the exact same size. It's much better than a video simulation because we can actually walk through it, so we know exactly how long it will take to get from the perimeter, say, to the building where Belle is being held and can time diversionary attacks, demolitions or whatever we need to coincide with.'

He looked around and everyone was nodding in agreement. 'Now as I told you earlier, the plan is to infiltrate by a ULL jump using one of the C141s that I've recently been jumping from at Fort Benning in Georgia. C141s are not only much faster aircraft than Hercs, but, since C141s are also routinely used by commercial airlines, it will be much less likely to attract unwelcome attention than a purely military aircraft like a Herc. We would normally plan to do the jump just before nightfall, giving us the cover of darkness to sort ourselves out and move away from the DZ towards the target. However, since dusk is the time that all the wild animals begin coming out to hunt for prey, we'll be much safer planning the drop for just after dawn, when all those animals have fed and are heading back to their lairs to rest up through the day. On landing we will RV, but we will then navigate to the next RV and ultimately to the target individually, except for Doc, who'll be with me.'

'I can go it alone too,' Doc interrupted. 'I can map-read, I learned that at Sandhurst.'

'But the SAS don't map-read,' Shepherd said, 'we navigate. GPS is unreliable in the bush or the jungle and anyway, if you're by my side at all times, that's one less thing for me to worry about. Sorry, but that's the way it's going to be.'

Doc bit her lip but stayed silent, while Shepherd was already wondering if he'd been wise to agree to bring her along. 'I will sponsor each RV,' he said. He looked over at Doc again. 'That means I'll arrive first and check it's safe for the rest of you to go there.'

'You don't have to explain every little thing to me,' Doc said. 'Even though I'm a woman, I was actually paying a bit of attention while I was in the Infantry and the Paras.'

Shepherd laughed. 'Fair comment, sorry, and from now on, I'll assume you know what I'm on about, but if you're not sure, please ask. So … each RV point will be chosen from the map and since we'll always be moving forward, each one will be closer to the target. When the job's done, we'll navigate to the LZ and be picked up from there by a Herc.'

'Won't any remaining enemy in the area hear the Herc and attempt to ambush us?' Doc asked.

'It's a fair question,' Shepherd said, 'but while they will hear it, they'll find it very difficult to locate it. I don't know if it's the Doppler effect or something else, but the noise a low level aircraft makes is somehow different from a heli. If you hear a heli, you can not only identify what type it is, but also track it to its landing site with relative ease. But with a Herc, you can hear it approaching and the different note of the engines as it flies away from you but, trust me, it is almost impossible to work out where it's gone.' Mr Angry and the Fijians nodded their agreement.

'To minimise our time at the Landing Zone, we've also arranged that the cousins-' he nodded at the Delta Force guys, '-will have a Herc on call somewhere in the general area for the duration of the op. So we can be picked up from the LZ within thirty minutes tops of sending out the burst transmission to say we're ready. The Herc will fly us to the Cape Verde Islands where we'll reconnect with the C141.'

'Why won't the C141 pick us up from the LZ?' Doc said.

Shepherd smiled. 'Because the C141 needs a lot more runway to land and take off from. Any other questions? Right, let's do this. All we need to do is zero our weapons - iron sights only, don't forget - and test the IAs: the Immediate Actions, how we react when we encounter the enemy or see a threat.' He broke off as he saw Doc's scowl. 'Sorry,' he said with a rueful smile. 'You already know what an IA is, don't you? Okay, last thing. As Stonewall said, we're going to need to make a river crossing and since it's likely to contain hippos or crocs, we're going to need a boat. So among the kit we'll be taking will be an inflatable dinghy. It's small - five foot by two and a half - so we'll have to cross one at a time. It's double skinned so it won't deflate quickly even if one of the skins is pierced and we'll use lengths of para cord from our chutes as ropes so we can pull it backwards and forwards across the river.'

Just before Shepherd drew the briefing to a close, he cocked an eye at the two members of the Counter Terrorist team who'd been carrying out oversight. 'Any comments?' he said.

'Just one,' one of them said. 'We'd like a piece of the action ourselves. Much better than sitting around here like spare parts, waiting for something that's probably never going to happen.'

'Sorry guys,' Shepherd said. 'I've already got my team, and anyway, if I pinch you from the CT team and a terrorist incident kicks off, we'll all be RTUed.'

CHAPTER 10

Shepherd and his team transferred by Puma helicopter to Lakenheath and boarded the C141. While the rest of them settled themselves in the back, Shepherd went forward to brief the captain, who looked more than a little nonplussed at being given orders by an NCO who would normally have been well below him in the military pecking order. 'Okay Captain, here's the plan,' Shepherd said, handing him the co-ordinates for the drop zone in the Caprivi Strip. 'You need to book a circular training flight from Lakenheath to South Africa and back. Pretoria, Johannesburg, Cape Town, any will do; it doesn't really matter which airport because we're not going to arrive there anyway. You'll obviously need a double dose of mid-air refuelling to extend your range enough beyond the normal maximum of 3,000 miles. When we're over the Southern Atlantic, you will claim that there is an in-flight "pressurisation problem" and obtain permission from Air Traffic Control to drop to low level and divert from the planned route to sort out the problem. You will then descend to low level - 300 feet - make the covert ULL drop over the Caprivi Strip and then, telling Air Traffic that you have only partially resolved the problem, you'll get permission to divert to the Cape Verde Islands and you'll then wait there until we RV with you.'

The Captain looked dubious. 'Ascension Island is much closer to the drop zone.'

Shepherd nodded. 'It is, but it's a military airfield and any op that has not been processed through the military hierarchy there will almost certainly be shut down by the base commanders, whereas Cape Verde Island is a civilian airport with a heavy traffic of tourist flights, so one more aircraft landing and taking off won't attract any particular attention.'

'And what are we supposed to do in Cape Verde while we're waiting for you?'

Shepherd's look suggested he was getting more than a little weary of the Captain's objections. 'Whatever the hell you like. As I said, it's a tourist area, so you can stay in a nice hotel, eat some expensive meals at Uncle Sam's expense, sunbathe, windsurf or take a pedalo round the bay if you want, just so long as you're refuelled and ready to fly at any time at two hours' notice. Oh, and one more thing: I need one of your crew to fit a compass by the exit door we're going to jump from.'

The pilot shook his head. 'There'll be no need for that, I can tell you the bearing over the intercom just before you jump.'

'Thanks but you'll be busy enough flying the aircraft at ultra low level without having to worry about that as well, so we'll do it ourselves,' Shepherd said, determined to make sure he had an absolutely precise compass bearing to help him RV with the rest of the patrol after the drop, and unwilling to trust the pilot to supply it for him.

Before they took off from Lakenheath, two of the hundreds of USAF tankers known as 'Kilo Charlie 135s' were already getting airborne from the Rhinemein airforce base in Germany and heading out towards the Atlantic to refuel the C141 on its long flight.

As soon as the C141 had roared down the runway on its take-off run and begun to climb towards its cruising height, Shepherd and the other SAS men lay down on the medical stretchers that the crew had installed for them and were soon fast asleep. Shepherd was used to ignoring the rumble of the jet engines, but he opened an eye as he heard Doc's footsteps on the metal floor as she paced up and down next to him. 'What's up? he said. 'Can't you sleep?'

'Sleep? There's too much on my mind. I'm surprised you guys can.'

'We can all sleep on a clothes line if we have to. It's one of the first things you learn on ops: sleep big and eat big whenever you can, because you never do know when you'll next get the chance.'

'Easier said than done,' Doc said, 'but I'll give it a shot.'

'Okay, good call.' He closed his eyes and was soon snoring gently but Doc was up again before long and she continued to pace up and down the length of the fuselage. The SAS men all slept through the first mid-air refuelling, but Shepherd was awake and alert as the C141 nosed slowly up towards the underbelly of the KC135 for the second refuel. The captain feathered the throttles slightly to bleed off a little more airspeed and eased the aircraft a few feet higher before guiding the fuel probe in the C141's nose into the drogue that was trailing behind the tanker. Once hooked up, the two aircraft remained in lockstep, flying at precisely the same speed and on the exact same bearing, with the C141 pilot on maximum alert, his gaze fixed on one wingtip of the tanker above and ahead of him as thousands of gallons of aviation fuel were transferred. If that wingtip dipped or rose even a fraction, he mimicked the move. There was a very limited amount of room for manoeuvre when the two aircraft were con-nected. If they diverged too far and the umbilical - the fuel hose - was ripped off, the C141 would be unable to refuel again and the mission would have to be aborted. The refuelling went without a hitch and when it was complete and the drogue had been withdrawn, the C141 flew on to the south while the tanker made a lumbering turn and began its long flight back to Germany.

Almost at once the captain of the C141 made a call to Air Traffic Control. 'ATC, flight 9740. Pan.

Pan. We have a decompression problem and need to descend to low level.'

'Roger that 9740. Clear to descend.'

The rest of the patrol woke as they felt the aircraft drop. Dawn was just breaking and at low level, beneath the radar ceiling of any of the missile defences and gun batteries available to Namibia's impoverished armed forces, the C141 turned east towards the African continent and skimmed in over the Skeleton Coast. The dense coastal fogs and ferocious surf had led many a ship to wreck there and so many mariners perished over the years that Portuguese sailors had christened the coast "The Gates of Hell". The C141 flew inland, over the vast sand dunes of the desert interior, one of the driest places on earth, heading towards the DZ in the Caprivi Strip. As they flew on, the desert gave way to typical African bush country of parched grassland, scrub and tall acacia trees towering a hundred feet above the plain. 'Don't land your chute in one of those Doc,' Shepherd said as they looked down on the landscape, the rising sun casting long shadows across it. 'Those acacia thorns are like hypodermics, only much sharper.'

She gave him a strained smile, her mind obviously fixed on the jump to come.

'We're all bricking it before a jump, Doc,' Shepherd said. 'And any lack of experience doesn't really matter because jumping from an aircraft doesn't get any safer, no matter how many times you've done it before; there is always the same risk about it, but as long as we don't land in a lion's mouth while it's yawning or splash down in a croc-infested river, we should be all right.'

She gave another strained smile and nodded.

The captain began counting them in towards the DZ and the team assembled by the exit door, with Shepherd keeping a close watch on the compass bearing. As always in these moments before an op in hostile territory, everyone was tense and silent.

The latest Go or No Go signal had just been received from Hereford: 'Knife and Fork' - it was 'Go'. A couple of minutes later, the Jump light clicked to green. Shepherd shot a final glance at the compass as the aircrew kicked the patrol's Bergens out of the door and then jumped back out of the way as the patrol exited as quick as a flash, only Doc hesitating fractionally before Shepherd gave her a push in the back and jumped out himself, hot on her heels.

In the old days of parachute jumps, aircraft like the C47s could reduce speed to as low as 100 miles an hour, allowing jumpers to exit the aircraft safely. More modern aircraft flew much faster and had a much higher stalling speed, so the ferocious slipstream would have prevented jumpers from exiting the aircraft at all. Modern aircraft like the Herc and the C141 were fitted with a hydraulic ramp in front of the exit door which would be raised just before a jump, diverting the slipstream away from that part of the fuselage and creating a near vacuum at the door that allowed the jumpers to have exited safely before the slipstream caught them.

As Shepherd felt the savage jerk as his chute opened, he shot a look around and was relieved to see the canopies of four other chutes deployed below him. Beyond them he could see that the smaller canopies of the chutes holding their kit, falling faster with only the minimal drag from the ten foot drogue chutes to slow them, were already beginning to impact with the ground. If anyone was watching from the bush beneath them, the white chutes they were using would show up vividly against the deep blue of the African sky, but military parachutes only came in one other colour - a green-brown shade - and that would have been even more prominent. Strangely and rather counter-intuitively, when jumping in low light conditions, the green-brown chutes were again more visible than the white ones. They showed up as dark blobs against the night sky, whereas the white ones barely showed at all, because the night sky was still visible through the thin white silk.

Shepherd shifted his gaze from the others and began to focus his attention on the ground, which was rushing up towards him. He used the risers to steer between two patches of scrub, then tensed himself and began 'walking' with his legs to reduce the impact as he landed and then thudded down into soft earth. As soon as he had hit the ground, he got to his feet, undid his harness and, having cut a couple of long lengths of para cord from his risers with his rescue knife, he got ready to discard his chute.

On most ops he would have hidden the evidence of his covert entry by simply rolling up his parachute and burying it, but in this terrain, wild animals would dig up anything he buried within hours. The same applied to body waste. Normally on ops SAS men would dig a hole to crap in and then fill it in to bury it, but in bush country animals would soon dig it up again, so digging a hole was a waste of time and energy and instead the waste was just left on the ground for the animals and the dung beetles to find and disperse.

Instead of burying his chute, Shepherd's options were either to hide it in dense scrub or lodge it up in the fork of a tree, out of sight of the ground. He chose that option, shinned up the trunk of an acacia, keeping well clear of the savage thorns, and hid the chute among the branches. He then slid down to the ground, checked his compass and began walking along the reciprocal bearing to the one he had taken before exiting the aircraft.

He found Doc straight away and was in time to help her dispose of her chute. There was a slightly larger gap before they reached Sam, caused by Doc's hesitation at the aircraft's exit door, but having found him, the other two were both only another fifty or so feet further on. They moved on at once, covering another 150 yards before coming to where the Bergens had landed. With only the ten foot drogues to slow them, they had fallen much more quickly and so were further away.

Shepherd then called a halt and took stock. There were a few cuts and bruises but no serious injuries and everyone was feeling the euphoria that always followed a successful para jump. They lay up for a couple of hours, watching and waiting in case their chutes had been spotted and reported to hostiles. They also used the time to check their kit and allow everyone to recover from the stress of the jump and the subsequent elation. As Shepherd had suspected would happen, the optical kit had not emerged unscathed and they now had only one working set of night vision goggles. The non-functioning one was discarded and like the chutes, it was stashed among the branches of another acacia tree.

Shepherd and the two Fijians worked their way outwards, checking the whole of the surrounding area for vehicle tracks or footprints. There were plenty of animal tracks, including the fresh prints of a leopard, but there were no signs of recent human traffic. While they were searching, the other two remained motionless, Mr Angry listening intently, having told Doc to do the same. Long experience had taught the SAS that in scrubby country like the African bush, you could often hear the sound of movement much further away than you could hope to see it.

After two hours, Shepherd called them together. 'Right, time to move out and split up,' he said. 'Doc will be with me, but Joe, Sam and Mr Angry will all travel solo. First RV will be just there at 1300 hours.' They crowded around him as he pointed to the feature he had identified on the map. 'I'm sponsoring it, so I'll arrive first to make sure it's safe and the RV will then be open for five minutes before and five minutes after the designated time. If anyone is running late but within earshot, the traditional monkey noise will alert us to wait a couple more minutes, but if anyone is still missing after that, the rest of us will go on to the next RV, closer to the target, and ultimately to the target itself, without them. And no matter what casualties we may take, the mission will not be over until the last man standing-' He shot a glance at Doc. 'Or woman - can't make it. So, just to be clear, even if there is only one of us left by the time we reach the compound, an attempt must be made to rescue the hostage, whatever the cost.'

The others looked at each other. No one spoke but there was no need to voice the thought that all of them shared. Their five person patrol was well equipped to achieve the task and the loss of one person should not be fatal to its chances. However, if their numbers were reduced below that, the odds against success would increase exponentially, and there was a two word description for what would happen if only two of them, or even just one, survived to reach the target: 'suicide mission'.

They set off at intervals of a few minutes, disappearing into the bush on separate headings. Shepherd waited until all sound of them had faded and then took a different route with Doc at his heels. He moved slowly, scanning the ground for any signs of people or vehicles and pausing every hundred yards or so to listen intently before moving on.

Behind them they kept hearing the snickering call of hyenas and the sound grew as the animals moved closer. 'They may well have picked up our scent and be stalking us, so keep on maximum alert; it's not just human threats we need to worry about,' whispered Shepherd.

They had been moving through the bush for a couple of hours when Shepherd found the fresh track of a vehicle in the dusty red earth. They moved on even more cautiously and then froze as they heard the sound of shots from close ahead of them. They moved forward a little more, but when Shepherd smelled the faint aroma of cigarette smoke on the breeze, he put his finger to his lips, motioned Doc to follow him and then dropped to the ground and belly-crawled forward.

Peering from beneath a thorn bush, he saw a group of men - four Chinese and an African who was clearly their driver and general labourer - in a clearing about twenty yards away. The Chinese were standing smoking cigarettes, watching the African as he lifted the carcass of an antelope into the back of their Land Cruiser. A cloud of flies buzzed around a couple of other animal bodies already stacked in there and Shepherd could also see two live creatures - prehistoric looking ground pangolins, with bodies completely covered in scales - that had been trapped and were now tied to the back of the Toyota's cab. Like the antelope horns, they were presumably intended for use in traditional medicine, while the dead animals would go for bush meat. To back-track and circle around them would have taken time that Shepherd could not afford if they were to make the next RV with the rest of the team, so he felt the only option was to take them out. He reassured himself with the thought that if the poachers had not attracted any other attention when shooting the animals, then killing the poachers now was not likely to either, particularly since the sound of the suppressed weapons that he and Doc were carrying would not travel much distance into the bush at all.

Two of the Chinese were armed with assault rifles - the Kalashnikovs found in their thousands in every conflict zone the world over. One of the others had a heavier calibre hunting rifle but the last one only appeared to have a pistol. The African was unarmed and Shepherd intended to spare him, if he could. He breathed in Doc's ear. 'I'm guessing you've probably never killed anyone?'

She shook her head.

'Well, I don't think this is the moment when you should be trying it for size. So be ready to fire if you have to, but to be honest, if I can't deal with these guys without you, then I'm clearly in the wrong occupation. The most immediate threat is the Chinese guy with the 7.62, so I'm going to take him out first.

The left hand guy with one of the AK47s comes next, then I'll take care of the right hand one with the other AK47, and finish up with the last Chinese who looks like he's only got a pistol. I don't want to shoot the African guy, if we can help it, because unlike them, he's on his home turf and unarmed, and he doesn't deserve to die when he's probably just trying to earn enough to feed his family. Anyway, with luck he'll leg it as soon as the shooting starts. Okay, you ready? When you hear me fire, that's your signal, not before.'

She gave him a worried nod, then slid her weapon along the ground in front of her and squinted down the sight. Shepherd took a quick look around the clearing to remind himself where any patches of cover or dead ground were - then moved sideways, away from Doc, giving them two angles of fire.

He sighted on the Chinese holding the 7.62, aiming for the centre of the chest - the percentage shot using the iron sights - then took a breath in and as he exhaled, he squeezed the trigger, twice. The suppressor deadened the sound of the shots to a sound that was no louder than a fist knocking on a wooden door and the rounds punched twin holes in the man's chest, the pink froth of aerated blood from his lungs mingling with the smoke trail as his cigarette fell from his lips.

Shepherd had already dived and rolled, coming up three yards from where he had first fired and blasting his second target apart with another double tap to the chest, even as a burst of return fire from the third Chinese man ripped through the bush where Shepherd had been shooting from seconds before.

There was no sound of firing from Doc as Shepherd burst from cover for a couple of seconds before diving into the shelter of a rock he had noted earlier. He caught a glimpse of the African driver sprinting away, then Shepherd focused on the third of his targets who was trying to use the Land Cruiser for cover but had left himself partially exposed. Shepherd sighted on the man's exposed left side and there was another Phttt! Phttt! from his suppressed MP5. The man screamed in agony as the first round ripped through his liver and the second tore away his left shoulder.

He hit the ground but although he was still potentially capable of firing, Shepherd now switched targets, assessing the last Chinese poacher as a greater immediate threat. He was crouching behind the Toyota's front wing, with the engine block protecting him from a shot through the bodywork, so Shepherd fired another couple of short bursts to keep the man's head down, then moved again, changing magazines even as he was diving and rolling across the dirt of the clearing.

He bellowed 'Doc! Don't shoot!' because he was about to put himself into her line of fire, then loosed off another short burst, dived and rolled again, and came up behind the rear wheel of the Toyota, diagonally opposite the Chinese man. Shepherd could see his hand holding the pistol and the top of his head from the nose upwards as he peered over the bonnet, trying to spot his adversary. It was all the target Shepherd needed. He fired again, twice. The second shot parted what was left of the man's hair but only because the first one had already done its work, smacking though his forehead in a brutal scalping that blew off the back of his head in a spray of grey matter and blood.

Shepherd heard a grunt of effort from the other man he had wounded and saw him trying to bring his weapon to bear with his one usable hand, but Shepherd did not even waste a further round on him. Drawing his razor-sharp rescue knife, he hurled himself across the two yard gap that separated them and slit the man's throat before he could even get off a shot.

Shepherd shouted 'Problem solved Doc, stand down', before emerging from cover, just in case she had overcome her stage fright and decided to get in on the action. He stood up and watched her emerge from cover, her face white and her mouth hanging open as she took in the carnage in front of her, while Shepherd checked his weapon and raked the surroundings with his gaze, alert for any sign of further threats.

'You all right?' he said. 'Don't feel bad about it, but I hope you've got the hesitation out of your system now. This time it didn't matter, but when we reach the target we're all likely to have our hands pretty full and if someone comes for you and you hesitate then, you'll be gone. So remember the drills we did with the 9 mil, shoot first and then think about it afterwards.'

She nodded. 'Okay, I will. I'm sorry.'

'Forget about it. No matter how much training you've done with live rounds, the first time in actual combat is a whole different ball game. Some people take to it like ducks to water, others freeze and some turn tail and run. You didn't do that, so you'll be all right.' He paused, checking her expression and noting that the colour was slowly returning to her cheeks. 'Okay onward and upward. The shooting will already have given those hyenas that were stalking us a bit of a pause for thought, but we can offer them a proper distraction now.'

The spare clips and ammo from the AK47s was 7.62 calibre and useless for their MP5s. There was no point in trying to take any of them with them, so he tossed them into some scrub. He disabled the Kalashnikovs by stripping them down and throwing the firing pins as far as he could into the bush. He then released the ground pangolins and watched them running off into the bush but he left the bodies of the poachers where they had fallen around the Land Cruiser. 'The hyenas, wild dogs and big cats will smell the blood and find them soon enough,' he said, 'as will those vultures circling overhead. So there'll not be much left of the poachers or the animals they killed for bushmeat, by the time they've all finished with them. Ready? Then let's go.'

They moved off into the bush again. As arranged, they briefly linked up again with the others at the chosen RV site in the fierce heat of the midday sun. All SAS men instinctively hated RVs, something buried deep in their psyche because the Escape and Evasion phase of their initial training meant that they had to be captured so that their ability to resist interrogation for twenty-four hours could be assessed. When on ops, it was the necessary amount of time for the remainder of a patrol or squadron to realise a member had been captured, cancel any planned RVs with him, and get out of the immediate area. At the end of twenty-four hours, the captive was released from his obligation to keep silent since he could no longer betray his comrades, and he was free to "bubble", to reveal everything to avoid further maltreatment or torture.

Since the whole point of E & E training was to avoid capture, the Head Shed always bubbled the location of one of the designated compulsory RVs to the hunter force chasing the trainees, thus ensuring that all of them were eventually captured and subjected to interrogation. As a result all SAS men developed an instinctive, ingrained mistrust of all RVs and approached each one with hyper caution.

Shepherd first circled right around the site, looking for tracks and listening for movement before allowing the others to come in. It was always an ultra tense moment for the sponsor of the RV because, with his senses on maximum alert, he would detect the faint noise and movement as people moved towards him, but would have no certainty that they were friends rather than foes, until they finally showed themselves. Some - and Mr Angry was one - were so hyper cautious that they would always take the RV time right down to the wire. If Mr Angry then mistimed it, he would have to hurry the last part or resort to the monkey hoot signal to show that he was in the vicinity but not yet quite at the RV when the allotted time expired.

CHAPTER 11

All of the patrol members arrived at the next RV within the allotted window and they were talking in whispers, exchanging information about things they had observed on their separate ways to the RV when one of the Fijians, Sam, suddenly put a finger to his lips and raised his other hand, cupping it to his ear, miming hearing something. At once all of them fell silent, listening intently. Among the normal sounds of the bush - birds, animals, the endless buzzing of flies, and the faint whisper of trickling water from an almost dried up stream - Shepherd could hear the slightest rustle of something or someone moving slowly and stealthily through the bush towards them.

He motioned Doc to get down, and he and Mr Angry took up firing positions while the two Fijians split up and slipped silently into the bush. Ten minutes passed with every nerve at hair-trigger readiness until there was the sudden sound of a scuffle in the undergrowth, the wet-sounding impact of a fist on flesh and a grunt of pain. A few moments later,

Shepherd heard the familiar monkey hoot call and Joe and Sam emerged from the bush, holding the arms of a young African man. His age was hard to assess but he was certainly no more than eighteen and might easily have been three or four years younger than that. He still had a well-worn AK47 slung across his back, showing silver where the original blueing had worn away, and there was a fresh bruise on his forehead from which blood was seeping.

They took his rifle from him and forced him to his knees, and he gave a fearful glance around the crescent of hostile faces in front of him, but his voice was firm as Mr Angry began to interrogate him. He spoke to him first in English, then Shona and finally, when neither of those produced a reply, in Xhosa.

The others waited as their captive gave a series of short replies to the questions Mr Angry barked at him, the language an incomprehensible mixture of clicks and guttural sounds to their listeners. Mr Angry eventually broke off and spoke to the others. 'He says he's with the CLF - the Caprivi Liberation Front. They're fighting a guerrilla war to achieve independence from Namibia. His home village was attacked by heavily armed white soldiers five days ago. They drove up in Land Cruisers, killed a lot of villagers including old people and children, raped some women, and stole food, fuel and anything else they could get their hands on, before torching the place. The CLF are out for revenge and he was patrolling, looking to pick up their tracks when he came across ours.' Mr Angry gave a bleak smile. 'And he thinks we're part of the same group of white soldiers. I told him they were our enemies as well as his, but I'm guessing he didn't believe me.'

'I can understand that,' Shepherd said. 'Given this region's history, every white man he's ever encountered in his young life has probably exploited him or brutalised him in one way or another.'

Joe bristled. 'Well, there's nothing white about me or Sam.'

'I did point that out as well,' Mr Angry said, 'but he thinks you two are mercenaries, taking the white man's dollar in return for helping us to kill our enemies.'

'So how far off is his main force?' Shepherd said. 'And how many of them are there?'

Mr Angry shrugged. 'He says - I quote - there are many, many of them, within a mile of here, but I'm taking both of those things with a pinch of salt.'

'Ask him how he communicates or RVs with the rest of them,' Shepherd said.

Mr Angry posed the question but they didn't need to speak Xhosa to gather that their prisoner was refusing to give any more answers. Leaving Sam to watch over him, the others moved out of earshot - just in case he understood English - and discussed what to do with him.

'It's an awkward dilemma,' Shepherd said. 'He's not our enemy, so we can't kill him, but we can't take his weapon and let him go either, because he'll probably bring the rest of his gang down on us and that's definitely an extra battle we can do without, particularly if the noise of that alerts the Yarpies. But if we tie him up and gag him so he can't shout for his mates to come and free him, he'll be food for the hyenas and wild dogs within a few hours.'

'He could be useful to us,' Joe said. 'He's local, so he might have knowledge of the lay of the land that could help us.'

Mr Angry gave a dismissive shrug. 'Maybe,' he said, 'but is that really worth the risk of dragging an unwilling captive along with us, who'll need constant watching and might give us away at any moment, given half a chance?'

'So is there a way of keeping him with us without him always trying to get away?' Doc said. 'Would money do it?'

Shepherd smiled. 'It might do. However I don't know about you, but I don't usually bring my wallet when I'm going on ops.' He thought hard for a few more minutes and then said. 'Hold on though, this might work.' He glanced across at the boy. 'What do you think his most prized possession is? The thing that in his eyes and probably those of his peers as well, makes him a man, not a boy?'

Joe broke into a broad smile. 'You've got it Spider. He'd give up anything before losing that.'

Doc frowned. 'What the hell are you talking about?'

'His AK47,' Mr Angry said. 'In our eyes, guns like that can be picked up for nothing - fifty quid or even less - but it might have taken the equivalent of a year's wages for this kid to have got his hands on one.'

Shepherd nodded. 'So that's the solution to the problem. Mr Angry tells him that we're not going to kill him but we're going to have to take him with us until we're nearly at our target. Then we take his AK47 off him and strip it down. That gives us six pieces. We'll let him see us bury the magazine in a place that he can find again and then we can set off with the other pieces.'

'And we should each carry one of them,' Doc said, 'so he can't snatch a bag from one of us and run off with his weapon.'

'Good thinking Doc,' Shepherd said. 'Yes, we'll do that. As we move along, we'll bury a couple of other pieces of it in places he can find when he back-tracks, so he knows if he sticks with us, he can get his beloved AK back again, but if he legs it and dis-appears into the bush, he's only going to have a few parts of it that will be useless without the rest.' He shot another glance at the sullen-faced boy. 'Okay Mr Angry, tell him what's going to happen, give him an energy bar to sweeten the deal.'

They waited while Mr Angry spoke to the boy. He was reluctant even to answer at first, doubt and hostility still clouding his features, but eventually he looked a bit less suspicious and began to reply. He took the energy bar that he was given but waited until Mr Angry had snapped off a bit of it and eaten it before putting any in his own mouth. He must have liked the taste because he then ate the rest of it in quick time.

'Okay,' Mr Angry said when he returned to the others. 'You'd be looking at him for a very long time before the words "willing collaborator" occurred to you, but he does love that AK and I reckon he'd walk to Cape Town and back to keep it. I've told him that we're not going to kill him and if he does as we say and doesn't try to escape, we'll let him go when we get to our target and he can then get his AK back. Even better, we'll be killing a lot of his white enemies for him. So, he told me his name is Jabari - it means courageous, by the way - and he's agreed to do as we tell him. He says he's never seen or heard of the compound we're making for, but I guess that's believable, because it's still a good few miles away and he and his comrades don't have vehicles and travel only on foot, so they won't usually cover too much ground beyond the area of their home village.'

They took the boy's AK47 from him, stripped it down in front of him and showed him where they were burying the magazine, at the foot of a distinctive acacia tree which had been struck by lightning at some time, splitting the trunk and blackening it. Jabari watched as they shared the remaining parts of his rifle between them, slipping them into their Bergens. Mr Angry then tied a length of para cord around the boy's wrist, just as an added precaution, and motioned the boy to walk ahead of him as they again set off.

Having chosen the next RV site, they split up again at once and came back together for the next one in late afternoon. The site was close to the banks of the river that they would have to cross - the mighty Zambezi, already broad and fast-flowing, even though Victoria Falls lay at least twenty miles to the east of them. The rapids were also downstream of them but at the point where they reached it, the river was a hundred yards from bank to bank and there were hippos wallowing in the muddy shallows at either side.

'We'll keep moving upstream until we find a safer place to cross,' Shepherd said, but although they walked a mile upriver, there were hippos or crocodiles and sometimes both, all the way. Shepherd eventually called a halt. 'We need to get across somewhere,' he said, 'and this place is probably neither better nor worse than any of the others we've passed.'

'If it's all the same to you,' Mr Angry said, pointing to where they could see crocodiles basking on the muddy banks, 'I'd sooner take my chances with hippos than crocs.'

'But more people are killed by hippos than crocodiles,' Doc said.

Mr Angry shrugged. 'Maybe so, but crocodiles are carnivores with mouths full of very sharp and pointy teeth, whereas hippos are herbivores with just a couple of blunt stumps to worry about.'

'And what sort of teeth they have won't matter when you're being trampled to death by a couple of tons of furious hippo,' said Doc.

'Anyhoo,' Shepherd said. 'We can't afford to waste any more time, so crocs or no crocs, this is where we're going to have to cross.'

They unpacked their tiny dinghy, inflated it and knotted together the long lengths of para cord that each of them had cut from their chutes making two tow-lines. They tied one to the handle at either end of the dinghy.

'Okay,' Shepherd said. 'Just one further small problem. Someone's got to swim that river holding on to one length of cord. Any volunteers?' There was no move from any of them to raise a hand. 'Well, no surprises there,' he said, 'looks like it's on me.'

Joe cleared his throat. 'No, Spider, I'll do it, but we'll just need to improve the odds a little first.' He stripped down to his shorts, dumping his clothes and his Bergen in the bottom of the dinghy, then picked up the 7.62 he'd insisted on bringing.

'Hold it,' Shepherd said. 'If you fire that, we're going to have to be out of here like shit off a shovel because we'll be sending out a very audible warning that our hostiles might pick up if they've got patrols out.'

Mr Angry nodded his agreement. SAS patrols always had a horror of making noise when on ops. It was why they routinely communicated in whispers, clicks and finger snaps, and if they did have to fire an unsuppressed weapon, they would take off at once, at top speed, trying to put as much distance between themselves and that area before the arrival of any enemy response triggered by the noise.

'But the whole point of bringing this was to use it against the local wild life,' Joe said.

'I know, but only if it was absolutely necessary. If we were right in the path of a charging hippo or rhino, I wouldn't hesitate for a second, but we're not, so let's use a suppressed MP5 instead. Same result, but much less noise.'

'And a more difficult shot, because the MP5 has a lot less punch.'

'Sure but enough for this if we pick a croc on this side of the river and go for an eye or the underbelly. Here, you get ready, I'll take the shot.'

Shepherd rested the barrel of his MP5 on a thick branch and sighted along it towards the biggest crocodile he could see, lying half-submerged in the shallows about twenty yards away. He lined up the iron sight on the crocodile's eye, took a deep breath, exhaled and squeezed the trigger. The silenced shot, barely audible above the noise of the river, was perfect, drilling straight through the crocodile's eye. As it reared, tail lashing in its agony, Shepherd fired again at the exposed underbelly, the round punching a fist-sized hole through the croc's hide and exiting on the far side, taking a mass of blood and entrails with it.

As the big croc thrashed around in its death throes, every one of the surrounding crocs, smelling the blood, zeroed in on it and began ripping its body apart in a feeding frenzy that even caused the normally unflappable Shepherd to suppress a shudder.

While the rest of them were watching the carnage, Joe had already dived into the muddy water upstream of the mass of crocodiles and was making for the far bank, thrashing through the water like an Olympic freestyle champion. He hauled himself out, mimed mopping his brow in relief, and then began pulling on the rope. Sam made the first crossing in the little dinghy, casting a nervous eye down stream at the crocs as he did so. He then took up a defensive position while Shepherd hauled on the other rope to pull the dinghy back and then Mr Angry, Jabari, Doc and finally Shepherd himself were hauled across. By the time they had finished, the feeding frenzy was over, all trace of the big croc had disappeared and the others had resumed their vigils on the bank or in the shallows.

'If we have to come back this way, someone else can do the swim,' Joe said with a grin as they deflated the dinghy and hid it in some dense undergrowth close to the river bank.

'No thanks, Shepherd said. 'A lift out by a Herc from the LZ sounds like a much more attractive proposition.'

CHAPTER 12

Dusk was now rapidly falling but they found a safe lying-up place, a cluster of boulders at the foot of a cliff, where one of them could remain on watch for the approach for prowling animals - or humans - while the rest got some sleep. They ate some of their dry rations and drank some water. Three of them then lay down in their sleeping bags and got what rest they could while Sam kept an eye on Jabari and Shepherd took the first stint on watch.

Joe, Sam and Mr Angry took turns on watch during the rest of the night and then around dawn they ate some dry rations and drank a little more water, buried another part of Jabari's AK47 in a place he could find again and then split up to make their way to the next RV, with Doc again tracking Shepherd, while Mr Angry once more took charge of Jabari, since he was the only one who could speak his language.

Their route now took them through the southern fringes of a dry forest that extended all the way north to the horizon, with tall, evergreen *mukwe* trees towering above the dense carpet of moss and creepers beneath them. Shepherd slowed his progress still more as they passed through it, for the trees and undergrowth restricted his vision considerably and though he had the skill learned in jungle training of being able to look through rather than at the outer layers of foliage, he was still even more reliant than before on listening for potential dangers - both animal and human. After four or five hours of painfully slow progress, the forest began to thin out and before long they were back in the familiar bush terrain: patches of bare, red dirt soil, dry grasslands and scrub, punctuated by tall thorn trees.

Their next RV was a couple of hours before dusk, only a mile short of the target. Having RVed, they were now close enough to the target and far enough away from Jabari's gang to be certain that he would not have time to alert them and return mob-handed with them before they had completed the op and been lifted out. So Mr Angry untied the para cord from around Jabari's wrist and they handed him the remaining parts of the Kalashnikov that they still had with them. Each of them then shook hands with him in turn and they watched as he set off back down the way they had come. He paused to look back after walking a hundred yards or so, and raised a hand in farewell, showing a gap-toothed smile as he did so, but then turned and was soon lost to sight as he headed on through the bush, back-tracking unerringly along the route they had followed.

This time all five of them stayed together as they walked the last mile in towards the target, with Shepherd working as lead scout, Sam and Mr Angry sandwiching Doc in the middle and keeping watch to either side of the patrol, while Joe was Tail End Charlie, keeping a careful eye on their rear. Moving at a snail's pace, working from one patch of cover to the next, and with frequent pauses to watch and listen, it took them almost two hours to cover that one mile, and it was almost dark by the time Shepherd had identified a site and set up an Observation Post on a rocky outcrop overlooking the compound. The others had meanwhile found a nearby place where they could lie up until the assault began. They stood to until an hour after sunset and then, while Sam, Doc and Mr Angry rested, Joe took the first turn on guard duty at the lying up place, remaining hyper watchful in case the enemy had decided to mount a night patrol outside the compound.

Shepherd took the first shift at the OP himself. He found the compound to be unaltered from the satellite imagery of it that they had studied in the pre-op briefing. Sentries with AK47s were stationed on low towers at two corners of the compound, and there was another guard by the gate to the compound, a steel mesh barrier in a very solid steel frame. There was some movement inside the compound, which was dimly lit by arc lights powered by a Honda generator, but the traffic was mainly men going to and from the ablutions block. However at about eleven, just as the place was quietening down for the night, he saw two white soldiers emerge from the compound's central building holding a young black woman by the arms. They were half-dragging and half-supporting her as she stumbled across the compound and disappeared into the ablutions block. They reappeared a couple of minutes later and ushered her back to the main building. Shepherd nodded to himself. His main worry had been that Kesia would already have been moved to a different location as kidnappers often did; in the Middle East it was rare for a victim to spend more than a single night in the same place. However, whether from carelessness or overconfidence, the Yarpies had evidently kept her here since the kidnapping. It was a big relief, the gruelling trek the patrol had made to the target had not been in vain.

They kept up a watch from the OP through the rest of the night, all the next day and deep into the following night, noting the enemy forces' routine, their comings and goings, and calculating the numbers that would have to be dealt with, and the probable locations within the compound where they would be found when the attack finally began.

Only once had the steel gates been opened as two Land Cruisers left the compound and drove north towards the training area. They returned a couple of hours later and each of them now contained half dozen African captives who were bound by the wrists and linked together by ropes around their necks. Once inside the compound, the Africans were dragged out of the Land Cruisers at gunpoint and then lined up in a row, face down in the dirt. The Yarpies then forced them to take up a position as if they were about to do press-ups and then made them stay in that very stressful stance. They remained there for over half an hour in the full heat of the burning sun and by then many of them were close to collapse, their arms and legs shaking violently with the strain. Eventually one of them fell face down in the dirt.

At once two of the Yarpies picked him up and dragged him round behind the main building, out of sight of the others but still within Shepherd's vision from his vantage point. He saw them knock their prisoner out cold with a vicious blow to the head from the butt of one of their rifles. One of them gagged the captive in case he regained consciousness and the other Yarpie fired a shot in the air. The two of them then strolled back round to the remaining terrified captives. Inevitably, one after another, the remaining men weakened and then collapsed, and the brutal charade was played out over and over again. Eventually only two remained. They were then pulled up by the hair, slapped and punched and then interrogated, with the clear threat that they too would be shot if they remained silent. Convinced that all their comrades had already been killed, they both began gabbling out any information they had.

When the Yarpies were satisfied that their captives had no more information to give, they dragged them round to the back of the building and showed them their comrades. Shepherd could not hear what the Yarpies were saying to the men and wouldn't have understood it if he had, since they were talking to the Africans in their own tongue, but the body language of the two prisoners and of their bound and gagged comrades, several of whom had now regained consciousness, showed that, out of pure sadism, the Yarpies were making sure that they knew the two men had betrayed them.

Two of the other captives had been given such savage blows to the head that they must have haemorrhaged and died from them, because they were left lying in the dirt. The others were untied, and pushed out of the gates of the compound. Shepherd was a little surprised that they had been released rather than being killed, but he guessed that if the Yarpies' aim was to spread terror in the local population, then sending them back to tell the story of their torture and spread fear among their villages might have been more effective.

Disoriented and chronically dehydrated the captives began to shuffle away from the gates and the Yarpies then sped them on their way by firing rounds at their feet. Even so, despite their terror, the Africans did not take the direct route away from the gates but stumbled and ran in the tyre tracks of the vehicles which indicated that the area was heavily mined. He noted with keen interest the way the Yarpies had earlier driven out of the compound and returned to it.

In both cases, the drivers had slowed to a crawl and then taken a curious zig-zagging route over the last hundred yards when driving away from, and back to the gates. 'There's only one logical conclusion we can draw from that,' he said to the others, as he briefed them about it that evening. 'They must have laid Claymore mines on the approach to the gates. I couldn't see any obvious markers to guide us and in any case we're going to be approaching in the dark with only one set of night vision goggles between us so it would be courting suicide to try to blow the gates and enter that way.'

'How do we know they haven't completely surrounded the compound with mines?' Mr Angry said.

'We don't,' Shepherd said, 'but there is thick scrub vegetation covering most of the ground around it and I could see animal tracks on the open areas between it, so if we follow the line of those, I'm confident that we won't be triggering any mines.'

Doc shot a quick glance at the others, but their faces remained impassive. There was a risk in everything they did on ops, and it was always a matter of calculating the acceptable level of risk and doing what they could to minimise it but never at the cost of jeopardising the success of the op or abandoning it altogether.

CHAPTER 13

Shepherd took the final spell in the OP up to four the following morning. The two sentries had already been on duty there for a considerable time - since eight the previous evening - and they looked much less than fully alert. He wormed his way backwards from the lip of the outcrop and slipped away to give the final brief to the others before the assault.

'Okay,' he said, his voice little more than a murmur. 'Joe and Sam will set a full charge on the wall of the ablutions block and another on the wall of the accommodation block. I will set a half-charge on the perimeter wall at the point where I, Mr Angry and Doc will enter. Once the charges detonate, we'll sprint through the breach in the walls and spearhead the attack on the remaining building, making entry using flash bangs where necessary and clearing each room of threats. While Joe and Sam give covering fire and engage any Yarpies outside the building, Doc will follow hot on the heels of me and Mr Angry. Her role is simply to extract Belle once she has been located, and only get involved in the shooting if she or Belle comes under direct attack. All clear? Then let's do it.'

The assault on the compound was scheduled to begin half an hour before first light, the time when the human body was always at its lowest ebb and the defenders would be at their least alert. While Shepherd and Mr Angry covered them with their suppressed MP5Ks, the two Fijians, Joe and Sam, crawled through the bush surrounding the compound and fixed standard charges to the outer walls of the two buildings on the edge of the compound: the accommodation and ablutions blocks. The charges had a self-adhesive backing, so the Fijians merely had to peel off the backing sheet and stick the charges to the brickwork, using an electrical initiation set to detonate them when they received Shepherd's signal. Each charge was more than powerful enough to demolish the building and anyone inside it. They then crept back to their starting positions, ready to go.

Shepherd fixed a charge to the compound wall. Since it was only necessary to breach the wall, he used half a standard charge, three quarters of a pound of PE.

Since they had no comms between them, the first shots would be the signal to launch the attack.

Just before zero hour, a sleepy-eyed white soldier emerged from the building in the middle of the compound, yawned and scratched himself and then shuffled across the bare earth and disappeared into the ablutions block. Shepherd shrugged. There was no reason to delay the assault, it just meant that there would be one less Yarpie to deal with inside the building.

Joe and Sam took out the two sentries in the towers, drilling twin holes in their chests with rounds from their suppressed MP5s without either of the sentries even raising his rifle, let alone getting off a shot. Simultaneously Mr Angry took care of the sentry at the gate, and the near silent phttt! phttt! phttt! of the three weapons did not disturb the sleeping enemies inside the compound. The first sign they had that they were under attack was when the charges were initiated. The man in the ablutions block must have heard the muffled shots or the thud as one of the guards tumbled over the rail of his guard tower and slumped to the ground. Still struggling to pull up his trousers, he came stumbling out through the doorway of the ablutions block, but was then torn to shreds by the blast and the flying debris, as the full standard charge on the outer wall went off with a sound like a clap of thunder, razing the building to the ground. The other full charge detonated simultaneously and the accommodation block was also destroyed. The rebel soldiers sleeping there all died instantaneously, ripped apart by the explosion itself or killed by the over-pressure from the blast that collapsed their lungs like burst paper bags, while broken brick, shards of glass and other debris were sent flying across the compound.

A heartbeat later, the half standard charge on the perimeter wall went off. Shepherd, Mr Angry and Doc had flattened themselves against the wall at either side, but as soon as it detonated, without even waiting for the smoke and dust to clear, they went racing through the gap the blast had created, stumbling on the rubble but then sprinting across the open ground to the central building.

Shepherd smashed the window alongside the door with the butt of his MP5 and tossed a flash bang through the hole. Mr Angry kicked the door down and both men went diving and rolling through the door, cutting down a couple of defenders, still with sleep in their eyes and struggling to identify the fast-moving threat, let alone bring their weapons to bear. There were two double taps, the second so close on the heels of the first that it might have been an echo, except that the two men had both been opened up like cans of beans, with the twin rounds, fired at very close range, tearing holes in their chests as the impacts slammed them back against the walls. Both slumped to the ground, leaving bloody trails down the walls as they did so, but neither Shepherd nor Mr Angry spared them a second glance, already focusing on the next potential threat.

There were rooms opening off either side of the entrance hall and Shepherd and Mr Angry split up, with Mr Angry going left while Shepherd and Doc, following in his footsteps, went right, clearing each room in turn. Both men had practised these drills countless times in the Killing House at Stirling Lines in Hereford - the building in which every room was draped from floor to ceiling with thick heavy sheets of rubber that allowed live rounds to pass through them, but stopped ricochets from penetrating back into the rooms. So many thousands of rounds were fired in there that the rubber sheets had to be replaced regularly.

Doc kept following a couple of paces behind Shepherd, her own weapon gripped in her hands though she had yet to have an opportunity to use it, so rapid and lethal was the force that Shepherd was using. He and Mr Angry had done the drills so many times they could have done them in their sleep - Mr Angry even claimed he sometimes did - and they had also carried them out for real on several operations, so they went about their work with a calm, unhurried but ruthless efficiency.

Several rooms turned out to be empty, but those that weren't were cleared with brutal speed. Several hostiles came running out into the corridor and were dispatched efficiently. A couple of doors remained closed and as he approached each of those, Shepherd kicked them open and tossed in a flash bang to momentarily stun and disorient any occupants. In case anyone was sighting on the doorway, ready to unleash a burst of fire into his chest, he then dived and rolled through it, identifying the prime target and taking him out with a double tap even as he was still in motion across the floor, then firing and rolling again or springing to his feet to deal with any secondary targets with equally deadly force.

While the sound of the shots was still echoing, he was already moving on to the next room. Doc was still a couple of paces behind him, her MP5 at the ready. Through the ringing of his ears, Shepherd could hear the rhythm of shots and an isolated blast from a flash bang as Mr Angry cleared the other side of the building, the detonation of the stun grenade followed a heartbeat later by the signature twin echo of a double tap, the shots so close together that the sound seemed to merge into a single detonation.

As Shepherd was approaching the last room in the building, there was a noise behind them, and Doc dropped into a crouch sighting her MP5 on a bend in the corridor, her finger tightening on the trigger, when Mr Angry appeared, shouting a warning as he came. Doc lowered her weapon, stifling what she was surprised to realise was a feeling of disappointment that she hadn't had the chance to put a couple of rounds into an enemy.

'The other side's clear,' Mr Angry said. 'No sign of Belle.'

'Then she must be in there,' Shepherd said, nodding towards the closed door of the last room in the corridor. 'And I'm guessing she isn't alone. Doc, wait there and deal with any fresh arrivals. Mr Angry, you get the door, and I'll sort out the welcoming committee.'

Doc and Mr Angry did as they were told as he moved silently forward, measuring each footfall, and took up position just past the door. Almost without thinking about it, Shepherd had already carried out the necessary observation of the door. He noted the position of the handle, then looked for the hinges on the opposite side of the door. If he could see the hinges, he would know that the door would open out-wards. If he could not - as was now the case - then he knew that the door would open inwards. He then waited with his MP5 trained on the centre of the door, bracing himself for what was to come.

On the face of it, launching yourself through a doorway into a room where one or more hostiles armed with weapons were waiting for you, was a near-suicidal move, but Shepherd had trained and done combat operations in these situations so often that he was confident that the split-second delay before the enemy reacted to his entry, was all the time he needed. They might well fire at the doorway where he had appeared, but by then Shepherd would already be away from it, inside the room, moving fast and beginning to take out his targets with double taps while they were still trying to bring their weapons to bear on him.

Mr Angry had moved up the corridor behind him and was now stationed on the opposite side of the door, nearest to the handle. Shepherd gave a silent Three - Two - One countdown with his fingers and Mr Angry gave the door a savage boot. The frame creaked and splintered a little but the lock held and a ferocious burst of fire from inside the room tore through the door panels about four feet above the ground. Mr Angry had swayed back out of the way after booting the door, but had either he or Shepherd been standing in front of it, they would have been cut to pieces.

Not knowing where Kesia was within the room, Shepherd was forced to hold his fire, but the burst from inside the room had torn a jagged hole in the door, big enough for a flash bang to fit through it. He glanced at Mr Angry and saw he'd already had the same thought. 'Don't pull the pin!' Shepherd whispered. Flash bangs didn't kill, they disorientated, but there was still a risk of injury and he didn't want to do anything that might hurt the hostage. By throwing in the flash bang without pulling the pin, it would hopefully panic the hostiles without causing any damage.

Mr Angry nodded and left the pin in place as he dropped the flash bang through the hole. He jumped back as another burst of fire tore through the door, then gave the door another huge boot below the handle and this time it flew open. As it crashed back against the inside wall, Shepherd launched himself in a racing dive through the doorway, aiming for the opposite side from the hinges. Even as he hit the floor, rolled and sprang upright, he had noted where the hostiles and the hostage were standing.

Having taken in the situation at a glance, his first shots, a double tap, were fired at a Yarpie who had been holding an AK47, standing in front and slightly to the side of the other two occupants of the room. From Shepherd's position, they were out of the line of fire even if his rounds went right through the man's body, and he didn't hesitate. The double phttt! of the shots was drowned by a burst from the man's AK47, but it was fired involuntarily by the spasm that seized him as Shepherd's rounds found their target. Both struck the centre of the man's chest within an inch of each other and the impacts hurled him backwards as his own fire drilled a pattern of holes in the ceiling and then fell silent as he slumped, dead, to the floor, the Kalashnikov falling from his grasp.

Shepherd had dived and rolled again to avoid any return fire and then sprang up and swung the barrel of his MP5 to cover the place where the other two occupants of the room were standing. One of them was Kesia, a look of sheer terror on her face. She was being held from behind by the other figure, the leader of the Yarpies, Johannes du Prez. His arm was around her neck and he was holding a pistol to her temple. Mr Angry had peered around the splintered door jamb and then moved to stand framed in the doorway, his weapon also trained on du Prez.

'Looks like a Mexican stand-off to me,' du Prez said, his thick Afrikaner accent almost burying the words. 'You can kill me of course, but I'll already have put a round into this thick black skull by then and I don't think that's going to play too well back in Washington, do you? Who are you anyway?

Delta Force? After Eagle Claw and Mogadishu, you Americans are already a laughing stock. Another fiasco like that and they'll be disbanding you.'

Shepherd said nothing, every fibre of his being focused on his target, waiting for a fractional opening, a momentary glimpse of part of du Prez's forehead that would allow him to make the killing shot before the Yarpie could make good on his threat to kill the girl.

'So what's it going to be, Yanks?' du Prez said. 'The rest of my boys will have heard all the explosions and shooting and they'll already be on their way here. You're going to have your hands full with them, so time's on my side, not yours. So you can run away now, go back to the US with your tails between your legs and tell your masters that the price of her freedom has now doubled or you can stay here and be killed - your choice.'

As du Prez was talking, Shepherd had noted the position of the unexploded flash bang that Mr Angry had dropped through the hole in the door, It had rolled a few feet from the door and come to rest against the skirting board. 'Actually, there is another choice,' Shepherd said. He whipped the barrel of his MP5 away from the target for a second and put a round into the flash bang. It penetrated the casing, struck the detonator running the length of it and the flash bang at once detonated with a thunder-crack, filling the room with smoke. Even as it did so, Shepherd's MP5 was once more trained on du Prez's head.

The distraction worked. The Yarpie's head swivelled slightly to the side, unable to avoid a momentary shift of his gaze to the source of the noise and smoke, and the barrel of his pistol lifted from Kesia's forehead for a fraction of a second. It was all the opening Shepherd needed. It had to be a head shot for an instant kill and du Prez had now given him a target. Even without the smoke now rapidly filling the room, it would have been a risky shot for most soldiers, but Shepherd was not most soldiers. He was SAS and had trained over and over again for just such a circumstance, knowing that he could guarantee putting a single shot into a target as small as a ten pence piece.

He squeezed his trigger, there was a Phttt! and the right corner of du Prez's forehead disappeared in a corona of bone fragments, blood and grey matter. His finger tightened convulsively on the trigger of his pistol and there was a crack as it fired, but he was already falling back and the round passed clear of Kesia's head and merely drilled another hole in the ceiling. Mr Angry added another double tap to du Prez's head and chest as he toppled backwards but it was simply insurance, for he was already almost certainly dead from the first impact.

The smoke from the flash bang obscured everything for a few moments, then it began to clear and through the eddies, Shepherd saw Kesia, frozen to the spot, next to where du Prez lay dead.

Doc had now appeared in the doorway. 'Doc, you're on, move!' Shepherd shouted as he saw her hesitate momentarily. She recovered and ran across the room and grabbed Kesia by the arm. As if released from her stunned silence by the movement, the girl now began screaming at the top of her voice. Terrified first by the gun at her head and then even more so by the shots that had passed within millimetres of her, she was now understandably in full on hysterical mode and could not yet be reasoned with nor talked down, so Doc had to drag her from the room.

Mr Angry had already run down the corridor ahead of them. 'Come on Doc,' Shepherd said. 'Any minute now, there are going to be more Yarpies round here than flies on shit. We've got to get out.'

They ran back out of the building, pulling the struggling Kesia along with them, but as they began to withdraw across the compound, Doc leading with the girl and Shepherd covering them, there was the sound of a vehicle engine being gunned and then a burst of fire. Shepherd swung up his MP5 to deal with the threat, then lowered the barrel as he saw Mr Angry at the wheel of one of the rebel Land Cruisers, hurtling round the corner of the building.

The original plan had been to walk out from the target to the LZ, but Mr Angry had commandeered a vehicle, which made more sense. He screeched to a halt alongside them. 'Why walk when you can ride?' he said with a grin. The Fijians ran up and jumped in the back with Shepherd, Joe at once settling himself behind the .50 Browning machine gun that was mounted at the rear, while Shepherd and Sam flanked him with their MP5s. Doc had pushed Kesia into the front and climbed in after her.

Mr Angry sent the Toyota screaming across the compound. It bounced and jolted so hard as it ran over the rubble from the blast that had breached the perimeter wall, that Shepherd, Joe and Sam were thrown around in the back and almost pitched over the side. They clung on somehow as Mr Angry gunned the Land Cruiser through the breach in the walls, the gap so tight that there was a scream of tortured metal as the door panels scraped along the remaining brickwork on either side. Then they were out, lurching and bucketing over the last bits of rubble from the blast and then roaring off into the bush.

Kesia was still sobbing, yelling and screaming, and Doc eventually gave her a slap across the face to quieten her down. 'We're here to rescue you, for god's sake,' she said. 'Now shut the fuck up and just do as you're told.' Kesia stopped crying and stared at Doc in amazement, unable to comprehend what had just happened.

'Know what Doc?' Mr Angry said with a grin as Kesia fell silent. 'We'll make an SAS man of you yet.'

'An SAS woman, preferably,' she said. Kesia burst into tears and collapsed against Doc, who put an arm around her and comforted her.

CHAPTER 14

As the dawn light strengthened, they were still bucketing through the bush but they became aware of two more Land Cruisers in hot pursuit. 'I put a burst through the fuel tank of the other Toyota inside the compound,' Mr Angry shouted, as he fought the wheel, 'so these must be the Yarpies from the training area north of the compound.'

His words were drowned in the din as Joe stood up in the back and began firing the belt-fed .50 Browning. He was struggling to stay upright as the Toyota bounced and jolted over the rough ground, but he had no choice: the machine gun could only be fired from an upright position. On either side of him Shepherd and Sam were keeping up a suppressing fire from their MP5s on the Yarpies, while return fire flashed past them, one or two rounds penetrating the bodywork with a thwock! thwock! sound.

Although the SAS men maintained a hail of fire, any aimed shots were almost impossible from the crazily lurching Land Cruiser. The pursuers were gradually overhauling them, laying down their own torrent of fire. Although it was generally less accurate than the SAS men's own bursts of single shots or double taps, they got lucky when Joe was hit by a round that smacked into his chest just above the small steel armoured shield on the Browning. As he slumped down, Shepherd jumped up and replaced him behind the machine gun, keeping up a stream of rounds until he had used up the last one on the belt, while Sam slapped a field dressing on to Joe's wound and then picked up his MP5 and resumed his own suppressing fire.

They were still about a mile from the LZ when there was a bang like a grenade going off as a round from the enemy Browning blew out one of the Land Cruiser's rear tyres. It slewed around, swerving wildly from side to side and throwing up fountains of red dust as Mr Angry fought to bring the vehicle under control, but just as he had almost achieved it, the opposite front wheel struck a boulder that was half-buried in the scrub, and the Land Cruiser was thrown up in the air. It teetered on the brink for a moment, the engine still screaming, and then crashed down on its side, with the chassis and sub-frame towards the enemy. As the bodywork crumpled and the windscreen shattered, Shepherd and the Fijians had been sent tumbling from the back by the impact and as the semi-conscious Joe hit the ground, the force of it tore off the field dressing over his wound, and fresh blood began pouring from it. Kesia, Doc and Mr Angry were bruised but unhurt and they clambered painfully out through the missing windscreen and crawled away into cover, dragging Joe with them.

Shepherd and Sam had meanwhile crawled behind the upturned Land Cruiser and began using it as a defensive position from which they resumed fire on the enemy. Now able to make accurate shots, Shepherd killed the driver of the first vehicle with a round that drilled a hole through the windscreen and neatly bisected his eyes. Sam then stopped the second Land Cruiser in its tracks with a burst that ripped through the radiator. A second burst caused the engine to burst into flames which rapidly engulfed the cab.

The Yarpies scrambled out of the inferno, beating at their smouldering, burning clothes with their hands. The others also abandoned their vehicles and took cover, then began to advance on foot "pepper potting" towards them. As the name suggested, the movement mimicked the offset pattern on the lid of a pepper pot. The first rank of troops would advance under covering fire from the second and then they would go to ground and give covering fire while the second rank moved forward in turn, advancing between the positions of the first rank and gaining a few more yards, before going to ground themselves. The cycle would then begin again, a steady advance that was hard to defend against.

While Shepherd and Sam gave them cover, Mr Angry sent the burst transmission to summon the Herc to the LZ, and then he and Doc made what speed they could towards it. Doc again took charge of Kesia, hustling her towards the LZ, while Mr Angry half-helped and half-carried Joe towards it. As they moved, they had to crouch low and dodge behind rocks and scrub as enemy rounds tore the air around them like swarms of angry hornets. The effort was making Joe steadily worse; he was again bleeding badly and his breathing was now very weak and ragged.

Shepherd and Sam were still keeping up their fire but they were now hard-pressed. The Yarpies had taken more casualties of their own but still outnumbered them and they had the heavier weaponry - the Browning on one of their immobilised Land Cruisers was still firing, although the sporadic bursts suggested they were running out of ammunition for it too. However, they were also firing AK47s and their 7.62 ammunition not only out-ranged the SAS men's MP5Ks but also had much more punch than their 9mm rounds.

The enemy were slowly fanning out, using the classic military fire and movement technique, trying to outflank the two SAS men and expose them to cross-fire. Shepherd squinted down the iron sight and drilled one Yarpie as he broke cover momentarily, sprinting towards a large rock that he was never fated to reach. The man's fingers convulsed in his death spasm, stitching a line of rounds from the last burst he would ever fire across an acacia, its arc marked by the whirlwind of leaf fragments, torn branches and thorn splinters it left behind.

Another Yarpie raised his head incautiously a fraction and fell back with a neat hole drilled in the centre of his forehead, its shape echoing the "O" of surprise his mouth had formed as he was hit by a round from Shepherd's gun.

Sam dropped another Yarpie on the other flank, as he tried to belly-crawl into position for a killing shot.

But despite these successes, the weight of fire on the SAS men only seemed to increase and the Yarpie forces were now dangerously close to outflanking them. One half-rose to toss a grenade at them but was cut apart by a burst from Shepherd that ripped a diagonal line from his liver to his shoulder. The grenade dropped from his grasp and, with the pin already pulled, it went off four seconds later, blowing the man's nearest comrade into eternity with him, as he frantically tried to scramble out of range.

As Shepherd ducked back into cover, an enemy round plucked at his sleeve and another came close to parting his hair. From the corner of his eye he glimpsed an enemy who was now almost level with him, and Shepherd fired in a heartbeat, but the Yarpie was already diving into cover and the round passed just over his head.

Knowing they were now outflanked, Shepherd shouted to Sam. 'Pull back!' The Fijian, his reflexes conditioned by thousands of hours of live firing exercises on the ranges and in actual combat, at once turned and sprinted back a few yards, then dropped

into cover behind some low rocks and unleashed a
ferocious burst at the enemy as Shepherd followed
his lead, hurdling the rocks and crashing down as
rounds whipped and buzzed around him.

The game of stealth resumed with the Yarpies
creeping forward again, taking a couple more casualties but once more on the brink of outflanking them.
Both SAS men were now very short of ammunition
and for the first time in his military career - in fact for
the first time in his whole life - Shepherd was having
to come to terms with the grim thought that this was
a fight that he might not survive.

He had barely assimilated that thought when, in
the next instant, the earth in front of them erupted.
Trees were shredded and torn apart, and there was a
succession of deafening crumps and blasts as bombs
and rockets streaked down from the sky. The Yarpies'
positions simply disappeared from sight in a mael-
strom of fire and smoke, dust and flying rock fragments as if a volcano was erupting.

As Shepherd and Sam flattened themselves in
the dirt, their ears ringing from the ear-splitting,
bowel-loosening din, shrapnel filled the air above
them and the enemy soldiers and their vehicles were
simply obliterated. The torrent of fire from bombs,
rockets, rotary cannon and machine guns continued for over five minutes and then died slowly away,
although flares and chaff continued to fill the air
to decoy away any infra-red ground to air rockets
that the enemy might still have been able to fire,

had any of them somehow managed to survive the holocaust.

Shepherd and Sam were already first crawling and then sprinting away from the battle zone towards the LZ. 'What the fuck was that?' Mr Angry said, gazing past them as they ran up, MP5 poised to take out any pursuers.

Shepherd only just heard him through the ringing in his ears. 'I'd say an Alpha Charlie 130 - a Yank C130 Herc gunship - wouldn't you? They're based in Florida with SOCOM - Special Ops Command - but with mid-air refuelling, there's nowhere they can't reach. A couple of them even flew a thirty-six hour non-stop flight to South Korea a couple of years ago, with seven in-flight refuellings along the way. And they've got more firepower than a squadron of tanks. You name it, they've got it: a 105mm howitzer, 25 mm and 40 mm cannon, Gatling guns, Hellfire rockets, precision guided bombs, infra-red sensors and a magnetic anomaly detector system that was originally used in Vietnam. It's so sensitive that it could detect the unshielded ignition coils of North Vietnamese trucks hidden under a dense jungle canopy, so finding a few Yarpie Land Cruisers in the African bush was never going to be a problem.'

'Well, I'm very glad the cavalry came riding to the rescue,' Doc said, 'but you can't fly here from Florida in twenty minutes, so how the hell did they know where we were or that we needed some help?'

'Delta had a watching brief and a definite interest in a successful outcome of this op,' Shepherd
said, 'so they've obviously had it patrolling in case
we needed a helping hand. And it's just as well they
were, because I don't mind admitting that Sam and I
were under some seriously heavy pressure back there.
Anyway, enough of that, how's Joe?'

'He's doing all right, aren't you Joe?' Doc said.
He was barely conscious and made no reply. She was
still on her knees, next to him, applying pressure to
a fresh field dressing to the wound in his chest, but
she turned to look at Shepherd and answered the
unspoken question in his eyes with a slight shake of
her head.

The next moment they heard the drone of an
approaching aircraft and a Herc came in to land,
rumbling and bumping down the rough grass strip
while the C130 gunship continued to circle over the
battle zone and fired another couple of rockets into
what was left of the enemy's Land Cruisers, though it
was hard to imagine anybody being able to emerge
alive from the inferno the C130 had created.

As soon as the Herc had rolled to a halt, the loadmaster jumped down with a stretcher. They lifted Joe
onto it, carried him to the aircraft and slid it onto the
Herc's aluminium floor. Their movements were gen-
tle but even that movement was enough to make Joe
scream with pain, and while the loadmaster secured
the stretcher, Doc injected a syrette of morphine into
his arm.

The rest of them had meanwhile scrambled aboard. The loadmaster shouted 'Go! Go! Go!' over his intercom to the pilot, and the Herc lumbered around, rumbled back down the grass strip and was airborne again within a couple of minutes, climbing as steeply as its engines, assisted by a Jet-Assisted Take Off Pack, would allow, while still punching out clouds of chaff and flares to guard against a possible missile attack.

The Herc was carrying a full medical trauma team - standard practice if casualties were expected among those being extracted from an op. They were undoubtedly a skilled medical team, but neither Shepherd nor Doc, nor the other two members of the patrol, would contemplate letting that team treat their patrol mate. They helped to set up a drip for Joe from the Herc's medical kit to get some fluids into him as fast as possible but they were otherwise left to take care of Kesia while Doc worked on Joe.

'I can't tell you how glad we were to see you guys,' Shepherd said to the Loadmaster. 'Your timing was perfect.'

The loadmaster grinned. 'It wasn't by accident, we've had an AWACS over the area for days. There seemed to be quite a concentration of enemy troops even for the SAS to deal with. So we thought you might be glad of a helping hand and put the C130 up on standby, just in case. The Boss held us back till the last moment because we didn't want to steal your thunder but, well, in the end, it looked like you could have done with the help.'

'Amen to that,' Shepherd said, but then hurried to the rear of the aircraft where Doc was still frantically working on Joe. 'How is he?' Shepherd said.

He had been drifting in and out of consciousness but when he heard Shepherd's voice, he muttered something.

'What did he say?' Shepherd said to Doc, struggling to hear above the low rumble of the Herc's engines.

Doc flashed him a tight smile. 'He said he'll never complain about malaria again, because this is ten times worse.'

'For fuck's sake, Joe,' Shepherd said, laughing despite himself. 'Will you can the jokes and save your breath for recovering?' Joe had already lapsed back into unconsciousness.

Doc kept working on him, doing everything she could to stabilise him and staunch the loss of blood by tying off the bleeders - the veins in his chest that had been ruptured by the 7.62 round. Sam knelt on the other side of the stretcher, his eyes never leaving his mate's face as he talked to him. 'Get through this Joe,' he said, 'and we'll go home together, mate, and never leave Fiji again.' He began muttering prayers for him in their native Fijian tongue.

Unfortunately Joe did not regain consciousness again. His breathing grew increasingly laboured and stertorous and his pulse was so weak and fluttering, that Doc could barely detect it when she pressed her fingers to his wrist. The pilot had just called 'thirty minutes to landing' over the intercom, when Joe made a noise that was somewhere between a gasp and a groan and stopped breathing altogether.

Doc at once began CPR and after a few seconds, Joe gave another gasp and began his ragged breathing again. It lasted no more than a minute and then there was another convulsive gasp and he stopped breathing once more. Doc again tried CPR and again Joe was jerked back into life, but Shepherd had seen it before in dying men. The will to live was a powerful force in anyone, let alone someone with the fitness and will-power that Joe possessed, but Shepherd knew that there could only be one end to this.

Once more Joe's breathing juddered to a halt and this time, although Doc yet again sprang up to do CPR, there was to be no further revival. The seconds ticked by, stretching into minutes. 'Save him, Doc,' Sam said, tears trickling down his cheeks and onto his massive chest.

She gave him a helpless look. 'I'm sorry Sam, I can't. He's gone.'

They landed at the Cape Verde Islands a few minutes later. They all transferred at once to the C141 and Joe's body was carried back to Lakenheath with them. A coffin had already been prepared and was waiting there when they landed. It was brought aboard the aircraft and they helped place him in the coffin and said their last farewells to him before the lid was screwed down and the coffin draped with the Union Jack and the Fijian flag, placed side by side.

Sam remained on board with him to escort Joe's body home to Fiji, for the traditional burial rituals without which, Fijians believed, his soul could not find peace.

The rest of them had disembarked and after refuelling and a change of crew, the C141 took off again at once, beginning the long flight direct to Fiji. Kesia, pale and still shaken, did manage a 'Thank you', to them before she was whisked away by a US Army medic for a more detailed examination before being transferred to another USAF jet, ready to be flown back to Washington DC and reunited with her frantic parents.

Shepherd, Mr Angry and Doc were picked up by a Puma and flown back to Hereford for the debrief that was required at the end of all SAS ops, not to apportion praise or blame to individuals but to assess the strengths and weaknesses of their strategy and tactics in the light of the way the op had actually unfolded and to absorb any lessons that could be learned for the future.

The three of them then said their goodbyes outside the briefing room. Mr Angry shook Shepherd's hand, hesitated and then gave Doc a peck on the cheek before walking away.

'Thanks Doc,' Shepherd said, 'we couldn't have done it without you.'

'Nice of you to say so, Spider,' she said, 'but we both know that's complete and utter bullshit. However, while it might be a little too strong to say I enjoyed it, it was a really valuable experience and I've come out of it with my respect for you guys even higher.' She paused. 'So what now?'

'Me? A spot of R and R and then back to the grind, I guess.'

'Want to start the R and R with a drink?'

He shook his head. 'Thanks Doc, but I'll take a rain check on that, if you don't mind. I'm beat and I need to get some sleep before I do anything else.'

She hesitated, her grey-green eyes fixed on his. 'By the way, Spider, are you married?'

He laughed. 'Why Doc, if I didn't know better, I'd almost think you were coming on to me.'

She flushed a little. 'Don't flatter yourself, I was just making conversation, though you know what they say: time spent on research is never wasted.'

'Well, anyway, yes I am married. She's called Sue and unlike a lot of the guys who are married but single whenever they're away from Hereford, I'm actually married full time.'

'She's a lucky woman.'

He smiled. 'So I keep telling her but she's yet to be wholly convinced about that.' He kissed her on the cheek, said 'Take care Doc,' and walked away.

Chapter 15

Shepherd had a brief period at home with Sue before being summoned back to take part in another op with his regular patrol and it was some months later that he bumped into Mr Angry while training at the PATA. Mr Angry had somehow managed to avoid being RTUed for the assault incident and by all accounts was keeping his anger issues under control. 'Have you heard about Doc?' Mr Angry said, as soon as he saw Shepherd.

'I heard she's no longer at Hereford.'

'Yeah, she didn't want go back to being a military GP and since the Head Shed still wouldn't let her attempt Selection, she quit and went back to the Paras. But that's not what I meant. They've just given her the Military Cross. The citation says she got it for "leading" the op to rescue a hostage.' He studied Shepherd's expression. 'Her only contribution to the planning of the op was to ask a couple of dumb questions. she didn't lay a charge, she didn't fire a shot. All she did was nursemaid the hostage out of there, after we'd done all the hard yards on the way in. Doesn't that make you fucking furious?'

Shepherd shrugged. 'It might, if it would make any difference, but we've both been around the Army block enough to know that's always the way it goes - Romeo Hotel India Papa: Rank Has Its Privileges. Since all medics are automatically given the rank of Captain, Doc outranked everybody else in the patrol, even though she was actually the most junior and inexperienced member of it. The Top Brass simply can't conceive of giving medals to other ranks like us if a Captain's been involved in the op, because to the Green Army way of thinking, if an officer's been involved, they must have been in charge. So if there's a gong going, under Army protocols, it has to be awarded to her, while the rest of the patrol, who actually did the work, get nothing at all. However, I know and you know, and more importantly, she knows, who really deserves the credit for that op.'

'And if there was any justice,' Mr Angry said, 'Joe Levula would be getting a posthumous MC or even a VC.'

'You're right there as well, but I reckon that'll be happening round about the time the Chief of Staff starts shitting rainbows.' Shepherd winked and strolled away.

ABOUT THE AUTHOR

Stephen Leather is one of the UK's most success-ful thriller writers, an eBook and *Sunday Times* bestseller and author of the critically acclaimed Dan "Spider" Shepherd series and the Jack Nightingale supernatural detective novels. Before becoming a novelist he was a journalist for more than ten years on newspapers such as *The Times*, the *Daily Mirror*, the *Glasgow Herald*, the *Daily Mail* and the *South China Morning Post* in Hong Kong. He is one of the country's most successful eBook authors and his eBooks have topped the Amazon Kindle charts in the UK and the US. *The Bookseller* magazine named him as one of the 100 most influential people in the UK publishing world.

Born in Manchester, he began writing full-time in 1992. His bestsellers have been translated into fifteen languages. He has also written for television shows such as *London's Burning*, *The Knock* and the BBC's *Murder in Mind* series, Two of his novels, *The Stretch* and *The Bombmaker*, were filmed for TV and

The Chinaman is now a major motion picture starring Pierce Brosnan and Jackie Chan.

To find out more, you can visit his website at www.stephenleather.com.

THE HUNTING

The new standalone thriller from the *Sunday Times* bestselling author of the Spider Shepherd series.

Can a doctor take lives instead of saving them?

British doctor Raj Patel puts his own life on the line to treat the injured in war-torn Syria. His medical skills help casualties survive against all the odds. But Raj needs to rely on a completely different set of skills when he is taken hostage in a treacherous case of mistaken identity.

Billionaire big-game hunter Jon van der Sandt is driven by revenge - his family have been killed by jihadist terrorists and he wants his vengeance up close and personal. He has hired ex Special Forces hard men to snatch the ISIS killers from the desert and transport them halfway across the world to the vast wilderness of his American estate.

But they grab Raj by mistake, and once the killing begins it's too late to plead mistaken identity. To survive, he'll have to become as ruthless a killer as the man who is hunting him.

The Hunting is published by Hodder & Stoughton and will be available in January 2021.

Printed in Great Britain
by Amazon